W9-CBX-821

THE BEST LIARS IN RIVERVIEW

THE BEST LIARS IN RIVERVIEW

LIN THOMPSON

LITTLE, BROWN AND COMPANY
New York   Boston

This book is a work of fiction. Names, characters, places, and incidents are the product of the author's imagination or are used fictitiously. Any resemblance to actual events, locales, or persons, living or dead, is coincidental.

Copyright © 2022 by Lin Thompson

Cover art © 2022 by Celia Krampien.
Cover design by Karina Granda.
Cover copyright © 2022 by Hachette Book Group, Inc.

Hachette Book Group supports the right to free expression and the value of copyright. The purpose of copyright is to encourage writers and artists to produce the creative works that enrich our culture.

The scanning, uploading, and distribution of this book without permission is a theft of the author's intellectual property. If you would like permission to use material from the book (other than for review purposes), please contact permissions@hbgusa.com. Thank you for your support of the author's rights.

Little, Brown and Company
Hachette Book Group
1290 Avenue of the Americas, New York, NY 10104
Visit us at LBYR.com

First Edition: March 2022

Little, Brown and Company is a division of Hachette Book Group, Inc. The Little, Brown name and logo are trademarks of Hachette Book Group, Inc.

The publisher is not responsible for websites (or their content) that are not owned by the publisher.

Library of Congress Cataloging-in-Publication Data
Names: Thompson, Lin, author.
Title: The best liars in Riverview / Lin Thompson.
Description: First edition. | New York ; Boston : Little, Brown and Company, 2022. | Audience: Ages 8–12. | Summary: While searching the woods that used to be their personal sanctuary, twelve-year-old Aubrey recalls the events and incidents preceding their best friend's disappearance and quietly questions their own gender identity.
Identifiers: LCCN 2021016153 | ISBN 9780316276726 (hardcover) | ISBN 9780316276993 (ebook)
Subjects: CYAC: Identity—Fiction. | Gender identity—Fiction. | Homosexuality—Fiction. | Runaways—Fiction. | Bullying—Fiction. | Forests and forestry—Fiction.
Classification: LCC PZ7.1.T46795 Be 2022 | DDC [Fic]—dc23
LC record available at https://lccn.loc.gov/2021016153

ISBNs: 978-0-316-27672-6 (hardcover),
978-0-316-27699-3 (ebook)

Printed in the United States of America

LSC-C

Printing 1, 2021

For everyone who's still figuring it out

PART ONE

A CONFESSION

SOMETIME IN THE LAST DAY OR SO, EVER SINCE JOEL GALLAGHER disappeared, I became a liar. I didn't mean to turn that way. I didn't even realize I was lying as I did it—not at first, anyway. Mine were mostly lies of omission. I lied by *not* saying things. These lies feel like a different category, if you ask me. They feel like something you just let happen instead of something you actively do.

But Father Jacob says lies of omission are still lies. They count with God just the same. Which is too bad, I guess, because the more I think about it, the more sure I am that even before Joel disappeared—even before *any* of this—I've been lying by omission all over the place.

It's Sunday morning now. Joel disappeared from the woods behind my house sometime late Friday night, or maybe early Saturday morning. *Disappeared* isn't the right word, but no one in town can come up with a better one. *Disappeared* sounds like a magic trick. It sounds like Joel just up and vanished, *poof,* from a patch of woods in the middle of Kentucky. There one minute, gone the next—like a miracle, but not the good kind.

"He can't have just disappeared," everyone in town keeps saying. But no one can figure out what actually happened to him, either.

Except me, I guess. I'm starting to have an idea.

Confession is a word that can mean a couple of different things. You can confess to the police about a crime you committed, for one: You can show up at the police station downtown and sign some papers admitting you're guilty, that you did whatever the police say you did. Joel and I used to put that kind of confession in our Secret Agents game. I'd play the bad guy who tried to assassinate the president or stole top secret information on a thumb drive or something, and Joel would play the agent who interrogated me and got me to crack. I'm surprisingly good at playing the bad guy. Joel is not surprisingly good at playing the hero.

It's against the law to lie to the police, and if the justice department in the state of Kentucky counts lies of omission the same way God counts them, I definitely lied to the police. I could make that kind of police station confession now if I wanted to. I could find the phone number on the business card Officer McCarthy gave me yesterday and call him up this morning.

But I'm not going to confess that way.

If you're Catholic, like Joel and me and pretty much everybody I know, you can confess in church, too. That's Confession-with-a-capital-*C*, one of the seven holy sacraments. You sit in a special room in the church and list off your sins to Father Jacob, and if you're really, sincerely sorry and really, sincerely plan to change your ways, Father Jacob will tell you God forgives you.

But I'm not going to confess that way, either. I feel plenty sorry about the lies I've been telling, but I can't go back and change them. I'm not about to tell everyone in Riverview the whole truth.

Maybe this is a different kind of confession. A confession that's not apologizing and that's not admitting guilt. Both of those confessions are the kind you make *to* someone: the first to a police officer, and the second to a priest. But I don't want to confess *to* anyone. That's the whole problem. None of them deserve to know the parts of the story I'm leaving out. Father Jacob, or Officer McCarthy, or Joel's parents, or my parents, or Rudy Thomas, or the kids at school—they don't deserve to know any of it.

The story I told about where Joel's gone, and about Joel and me and everything that led up to him disappearing, has been like a bunch of puzzle pieces whose edges won't quite line up. You can try to force them together, but the picture they make is jumbled and crammed. It's missing too many pieces in the middle.

This isn't a confession *to* anyone. It's a confession in the telling. I have to tell the missing pieces.

And I'm sure I'll have plenty more pieces to confess before this is all over and done.

ONE VERSION OF THE STORY

THE OFFICIAL STORY I TOLD TO THE POLICE AND JOEL'S PARENTS AND everyone in town about the night he disappeared goes like this:

On Friday night, Joel and I went out camping. We always go camping on the last day of school, the first night of summer. It's been our tradition since kindergarten. Joel and I have lots of traditions like that. Things we've done over and over for as long as we've been friends, which means basically forever. In past years, sometimes my mom or dad has joined us, or Joel's mom or dad, or my older sister, Teagan, or one year a dog the Gallaghers were dog-sitting. But no one else goes every single year. Just Joel and me.

This year, my parents were tired out from work. Teagan had decided she didn't like camping anymore unless it was inside a cabin with air-conditioning. Mari Clark-Espinoza, our new friend from school this year, had wanted to come along but had to drive to Louisville the next morning for something with her moms that Mari wouldn't explain any further. My dad said that Joel and I were finally old enough to stay out by ourselves, so he helped us carry our supplies to the same clearing in the woods we've been camping in since kindergarten, helped us pitch two tents, and then hiked home.

So it was just Joel and me.

But late that night Joel and I both got spooked. We know every inch of the woods during the daytime. We've crisscrossed them hundreds of times, over and over, pretending that we're pirates or spies or warriors or elves. We know how to make trail markers for each other out of broken sticks or rocks. We know how to tell apart the different kinds of birds. We know all the names of the trees.

But the woods at nighttime are different. There are noises, ones that in daytime I could probably recognize as just the wind through the trees or someone's dog barking. In the dark, they sound like bears or wolves or ghosts.

So we got spooked, and Joel and I decided that camping out with just the two of us wasn't such a good idea. We put out the fire and packed up the tents. I walked back to my house. I figured he was walking back to his.

Joel never arrived home.

That's the end of that version of the story.

A TRUER VERSION
OF THE STORY

HERE ARE SOME PARTS OF THE STORY I LEFT OUT:

1. The homemade raft Joel and I built together, hooked to the bur oak tree beside Mystic Creek, during the last two weeks of sixth grade.

2. Our many, many plans to run away.

3. The unrepeatable names Rudy Thomas and the other kids in our class had called Joel at school.

4. What Joel said about those names that night when we were camping.

5. The fight Joel and I had by the campfire that night, before he disappeared.

6. The look in Joel's eyes after the fight stopped.

Joel and I have been friends so long that I know every facial expression he can make. I keep a list of them in my head so I can name them as they happen—I like having categories for things. I like organization. There's his wide-eyed Begging Puppy Dog look when he wants something. There's the sideways smile of his I'm Up to Something look. There's the too-bright Cover-Up Smile when he's trying to act like he's not upset but really he is.

But his wild, reckless look after we stopped fighting that night—that one was new. I didn't have a name for that one.

A VIGIL

NOBODY'S BEEN SURPRISED TO LEARN THAT I WAS THE LAST PERSON TO SEE Joel. The two of us are always together. I used to figure Joel and me had the kind of friendship that happens because you're around each other all the time— because you're the same age, and you live in the same neighborhood, and you're in the same class at school every year, and your families have gone to the same nine o'clock Mass at the Church of the Sacred Heart every Sunday since forever and ever, amen.

Maybe that's how we started out. But Joel and me are more than that. My dad says we're two peas in a pod. My grandma Sadie says we're tight as ticks.

Teagan says we're the same kind of weird, and she's probably right. Joel and me, we're whole summers of playing our Secret Agents game and our Pirates game and our Woodland Elves game together in the woods. We're jokes that nobody else laughs at because they're only funny if you know the three different stories the joke is talking about. We're afternoons of lying side by side on the ground and flipping through all my Kentucky nature guides and never having to worry about saying something strange or wrong. Talking without having to think.

By now, it's impossible to tell if Joel and I have stayed friends because we're the same kind of weird or if we're the same kind of weird because we've been friends so long. I like to think of us like two of the tomato vines in my dad's garden, the ones that climb up around the same chicken-wire fence. We've been around each other for so long that we've grown up the same.

Maybe that was our problem this year. Sixth grade brought some good things, like Mari Clark-Espinoza. But it also brought plenty of bad, like Rudy Thomas and Vice Principal McDonnell and all kinds of new middle school social rules that I didn't know how to follow and that Joel didn't *care* about following. Maybe we've just gotten further apart.

Or maybe Joel and me stopped fitting together the way we used to.

That's what I'm thinking about Sunday morning, during our usual nine o'clock Mass at the Church of the Sacred Heart. Father Jacob has set apart this week's as a vigil Mass for Joel, which means we're supposed to be praying extra hard through the whole thing for Joel to come home safe. It's been a little over a day since we found out Joel was gone. As if I can think about anything else.

I've spent every Sunday of my life here in the Church of the Sacred Heart, kneeling on the fold-down kneelers the color of eggplant and staring up at the carving of Jesus on the cross that hangs over the altar. Jesus's hands and feet have little trickles of blood painted onto them, and his eyes are pointing up, I guess toward heaven. I've always thought his face looks almost bored, though.

It's after Communion now, and on the altar, Father Jacob is leading a special prayer for Joel. He's stretched his arms out and tilted his face up toward the ceiling, so he's in just the same position as Jesus behind him.

"Lord Jesus, please send your guardian angels to watch over our dear child until he's returned to us," Father Jacob is saying.

We're all kneeling down and are supposed to have our heads bowed, but I can't stop fidgeting and looking around. My dad's on one side of me; Teagan's on the other. Every so often, my dad reaches over and gives my folded hands a little squeeze.

Most of Riverview has shown up for Mass, or at least it seems that way. In front of us are the Millers, who live down the street from Joel's family and have seven kids. There's Mr. and Mrs. Fitzgerald, who are both about a million years old and always bring this really smelly jam cake to the church potlucks. Rudy Thomas and his family are here; they're sitting a couple of pews ahead of us. So is Parker Ferguson. Parker is leaning over and looking at something in his hand, probably texting out of his pocket. He mutters something to Rudy Thomas, and Rudy snorts out a laugh till Mrs. Thomas leans over and hisses them both quiet.

Riverview's the kind of town where you know pretty much everybody. Where the same families have lived for ages and ages. Where you get stuck talking to the elderly ladies from church for half an hour anytime your mom sends you to run into Kroger for milk. Even if you meet somebody around town who you haven't met before, you can both list off names of cousins and neighbors and church friends till you find someone the other one knows.

Vice Principal McDonnell is here, sitting between her husband and their two kids. Even Officer McCarthy, the police officer who's in charge of Joel's case, is here for the vigil. For a split second I think he sees me looking at him, and he gives me a nod, but I bow my head again quick and pretend not to notice.

"Please, Lord," Father Jacob is saying. "Please grant us your heavenly guidance to find our child safe and well."

That *our child* part bugs me. He probably means *our child* like Joel is part of our community. Part of the Church of the Sacred Heart. But it makes my whole body feels stiff.

"Please grant us your peace as we wait for Joel's safe return."

Now Father Jacob reaches out a hand toward Joel's mom and dad, who are kneeling in their usual pew right at the front of the church. They look wrong without Joel there in the middle. Joel's dad stays very still, staring straight ahead, his mouth pulled into a tight line. Beside him, Joel's mom is thrumming with energy. The left leg of her pants is jiggling up and down in exactly the same way Joel's leg jiggles when he's restless.

"Please grant your peace to April and Jonathan in this difficult time," Father Jacob says.

"That poor family," Mrs. Miller in front of us murmurs, and Mr. Miller clucks in agreement.

Joel's mom and dad don't need *peace*. They need Joel.

Father Jacob keeps praying, and Teagan bumps her shoulder against mine. When I glance over at her, she doesn't say anything, but she gives me a little side smile and bumps me again. On the other side of her, my mom is bowing her head, but she keeps looking over at Teagan and me every couple of seconds. Making sure we're still here, I guess.

After Father Jacob finishes his prayer, the choir starts up a hymn about God being a shepherd who looks after his lost sheep, and the ushers hand out candles to everyone, even kids. The candles are the same skinny white kind we light every year at Easter. Maybe they're the exact same ones, left over from last month. They have little paper cups around the middle to catch the wax as it melts.

We all pass the flame down each pew, candle to candle, person to person. Teagan uses her candle to light mine, her hand cupped up around the flame to protect it. After mine catches, I tip it over and light my dad's. He's singing with the hymn, his voice soft but steady. I try to kind of mouth along with the words, but any sound gets stuck in my throat.

My candle's melting too fast. The white drips of wax slide down its side. There's a little gap between the wax-catching cup and the candle, and a big glob of wax slides right through it and lands on the side of my hand, scalding hot. I don't move. I just sit there and watch it. I leave the wax there till it cools, and then I peel it off my skin and roll it up into a little ball. The skin underneath has turned a little pinker than usual.

"'God is my shepherd, so nothing shall I want,'" the choir sings.

It's not true, though. I want so much. I want Joel to be here with us in the church. I want everything to go back to the way it's supposed to be. I want to go back to the beginning of this year, or maybe even earlier. Back before everything got complicated. Before everything started feeling wrong. I want to be somewhere—anywhere—else, anywhere besides this pew in the Church of the Sacred Heart.

I just keep rolling my little ball of wax between my fingers. Joel and me have been friends so long, it's always felt like we're tied together. Like there's a string between us. Like when we made a tin-can telephone back in first grade. It didn't really work as a telephone—maybe we didn't make it right or didn't know how to use it. But I liked that telephone anyway.

I liked how I could hold on to one end and Joel could hold on to the other, and the long, long piece of yarn would run from him to me, connecting us.

Ever since we realized he was gone yesterday morning, ever since I found out he didn't come home from camping, I've kept trying and trying. But I can't feel that string anymore.

It's cut down the middle. And the other end is gone.

A CONVERSATION WITH JOEL'S MOM

AFTER MASS, EVERYBODY HEADS OVER TO THE PARISH HALL TO FORM A search party. We've prayed to God to bring Joel home, and now it's time for us to try to bring him home ourselves.

My family's heading toward the church's back doors when I realize Joel's mom has beaten us there. She's waiting just inside the doorway—waiting for me.

She and Joel's dad have already talked to me a bunch of times since Joel disappeared. They called our house, first thing yesterday morning, when they realized Joel hadn't come home from our camping trip. Then they both came over to our house to ask all the same questions in person. His mom had made me think of a hummingbird—fluttery and skittish, full of nervous energy but with nowhere to put it. I know that feeling.

Right when I spot her in the church doorway, my heart starts thrum-thrum-thrumming. *Run*, my brain says, *hide, maybe she won't see you*, but of course she does. She murmurs something to my mom, who nods, and Joel's mom pulls me off to the side. She tucks us in an alcove by the table of prayer candles, with a stained glass window of the Virgin Mary staring down at us.

Joel's mom looks as nervous as I am. She keeps clasping and unclasping her hands.

"I just wanted to ask," she says, then stops. Clasps her hands. Unclasps them. "I have to ask if there's anything else you can remember from the other night. Anything at all. I know how you two are."

How you two are. It's such a short way to sum up our whole lives together. Playing in the woods. Making up stories. Telling each other everything. Or at least, we used to.

Joel's mom looks a lot like him. Older, obviously, with darker brown skin and her hair in long braids, but something in her eyes and the curve of her mouth matches Joel's perfectly. She fills in the gaps that are always left when you look at Joel alongside his dad. Not just the obvious stuff, like his skin color and hair—Joel and his mom are Black while his dad is white. It's more than that. His dad doesn't smile very much, and his eyebrows always point down a little. Without seeing Joel's mom, you can't figure out where his joy and energy and heart come from.

Her dark brown eyes are so soft and serious now that looking right at them makes me feel like I swallowed a rock. I look at her shoes instead.

"I know he was having a rough time," she says. "His dad and I..." She shakes her head and tries again. "I should've...I mean, we were talking about..."

"He told me," I say, because I don't want to hear her say it. My stomach starts sinking into a pit that feels like it might swallow me whole. I don't want to think about what Joel told me by the campfire that night. I don't want to think about our fight. I shove my hands into my pockets and clench them into fists, pushing my fingernails into my palms. At least that hurts less than the sinking.

"I've started asking around," Joel's mom says. "And I know the police are trying. But if there's anything you think of that might be important— something he said, or someplace you talked about. Aubrey."

I have to look at her then, when she says my name.

"Do you have any idea where he might've gone?"

I guess I haven't really thought hard about the lies I've told up till now. I know they're wrong. I know *I'm* wrong. But it's so easy to leave the tough parts out. And I've been doing my best not to think too hard. Everything that happened on the last day of school—*Don't think about that*, I've kept telling myself. Our fight by the campfire. *Don't think about that.* Finding out Joel was gone. *Don't think about that.*

Yesterday morning, when I talked to Joel's parents, and later on, when Officer McCarthy asked me for all the details down at the police station, they had all asked, "Do you know where Joel is?"

And when the question is *Do you know where he is?* I can honestly answer no. I don't.

But when the question is *Do you have any idea where he might have gone?*

Well. If I'm being totally honest, I have a hunch.

Joel's mom is still studying me, staring right into my eyes. I try and try to swallow down the rock in my throat. To go back to before the lies felt like they really mattered. In my pocket, I can still feel the little ball of wax from my vigil candle.

"Sorry. I don't know," I hear myself say. "But I'll tell you if I think of anything."

As I cross over to the parish hall and meet up with my parents and Teagan, I try to convince myself I did the right thing. I *don't* know anything—not for sure. I shouldn't get Joel's mom's hopes up before I even find out if my hunch is right. If I tell her all the parts of the story I left out, I'll get in huge trouble, and Joel will get in trouble, and besides, maybe I'm wrong, and then even after all that we still won't be any closer to finding him.

But I know that's not the whole of it. There's another reason, too. An uglier reason. One that keeps

23

my stomach clenched tight for a long, long time. I'm not proud of it, but this is a confession, and the truth is that maybe I don't tell her because I'm mad at her. When I look at her, all I can think about is what Joel and I had fought about by the campfire that night. All I can think is *You can't just take him away*.

I'll wait till I know more, I figure. Then I'll tell.

But it turns out that's another lie. Later, after the search parties come back and show Officer McCarthy what they've found, I know without a doubt that my hunch is right. And even then, I keep my mouth shut.

A MEETING WITH A POLICE OFFICER

THE DAY BEFORE, ON SATURDAY MORNING, JOEL'S MOM AND DAD HAD filed a report with the police. That was the morning we realized Joel hadn't come home from camping. His parents called the police station from our house right after I told them my partial version of the story. Joel's mom kept pacing back and forth across our kitchen. Joel's dad sat with his hands cupped under his chin, his cell phone on speaker on the table. He answered all the officer's questions in a level voice with an annoyed frown on his face. I wasn't sure if he was annoyed at the police officer he was talking to or annoyed at Joel for causing so much trouble.

Since I was the last person to see Joel before he disappeared, the police officer on the phone asked if I would come down to the station to make a statement.

"Just to get the story in your own words," he said.

Joel's mom stopped pacing when he said that, and she looked at me with her soft eyes that made my stomach feel flippity-floppity, till I nodded and said okay.

My dad drove me to the police station that afternoon. The place was stuffy and hot. They had the heater running even though it's almost the end of May.

"How about you start at the beginning," Officer McCarthy said. He sat me and my dad down in metal folding chairs across from his desk. "Tell me about what happened last night."

Repeating the version of the story I'd told Joel's parents to Officer McCarthy was easy. He *hmm*-ed in some spots and *uh-huh*-ed in others, tapping out notes on his computer. He had a copy of Joel's sixth-grade school picture on the table in front of us—the same one the Gallaghers have hanging in the front hallway of their house. It showed Joel's brown face grinning and dimpled, his curls trimmed short, the collar of his blue-checked shirt crisp and clean.

The whole time I was talking, I stared at that photo. I tried to pretend I was telling the story *to* Joel instead of about him. But it felt just like that—pretending.

After I'd finished telling my story about the night before, Officer McCarthy leaned back in his chair and looked at me over his computer screen.

"I'm gonna ask you some questions," he said. "Just to get a sense of what else might be going on with your friend. Has he seemed different lately?"

Joel's *always* been different—at least that's what people say about him. It's their more polite way of pointing out that Joel just does what he wants and doesn't care about what people think.

I was pretty sure that wasn't what Officer McCarthy meant, though, when he asked that. "Different how?" I said.

"Acting funny. Like, unusually reckless, or secretive, or—"

"I don't think so," I said.

"He's seemed quieter," my dad added. He looked over at me a little sideways, like he was wondering why I hadn't spoken up about it. "At least to me." He'd picked up a paper brochure off a little stand beside Officer McCarthy's desk and was using it to fan himself. "We've been talking with April and Jon. With his parents. Seems like he's had a lot going on."

"How's school been going for him?" Officer McCarthy said.

My dad looked over at me again, waiting for me to answer. I rubbed my hands on my legs.

"Not so good," I said.

"Has anybody there been making trouble for him?"

"Yeah, I guess." What did he want—a list? Rudy Thomas. Parker Ferguson. James Todd. Vice Principal McDonnell...

"I saw there was some kind of incident at school yesterday," Officer McCarthy said, shuffling through some papers from the same file folder as Joel's school picture. He must've gotten them all from Riverview Middle. "Something about a pair of sneakers...?"

"After PE, yeah," I said. I didn't want to have to tell that part, but Officer McCarthy kept looking at me expectantly, so I did.

Officer McCarthy typed it all down. My dad kept fanning himself with the brochure, back and forth, making a *fwip, fwip* sound. He fanned hard enough that the breeze from it ruffled through my hair.

When I was done, Officer McCarthy asked, "Has Joel ever talked about hurting himself?" His cheeks were flushed red from the heat. He'd sweated through his uniform shirt in a T shape stretched across his chest. It was a big question, but the way he asked it didn't feel big. He asked it in the same easy, almost bored way he'd asked everything else.

"No, he hasn't," I told him. And that was true.

"Has he ever talked about running away?" he asked.

"No," I told him again.

So that was the first lie I said outright. Joel talks about running away all the time.

The whole thing felt to me like an interrogation. It felt like when I'm playing the bad guy in Joel's and my Secret Agents game. But Officer McCarthy kept saying we shouldn't worry. He kept saying this was all just a formality, that Joel would turn up soon. He figured Joel had probably just gone for a long walk without telling anyone or was lying low at a friend's house.

I guess he was trying to comfort us that Joel would be okay. But it scratched at me. It felt like he didn't really care. Like he didn't think that Joel being missing was that big of a deal. I thought about Joel's dad frowning, being annoyed instead of panicky or scared that his only child was missing.

My mom would say everybody deals with hard times in their own way. But I was pretty sure Joel's dad was dealing wrong.

Every time Officer McCarthy told us we shouldn't worry, it just made me worry more. Of *course* I was going to worry. Joel hadn't just gone on a long walk— he hates going on walks by himself, anyway. He says it's too quiet. And he wasn't lying low at a friend's house—besides me and Mari, he doesn't have any real friends to lie low with.

That's when I decided I didn't want Officer McCarthy to find Joel, either. He didn't even *know* Joel. He didn't get it. He shouldn't be the one to bring Joel back.

When the interrogation was over, as my dad and I

were peeling ourselves out of our folding chairs to go home, Officer McCarthy handed me a business card. His name and phone number were printed on it.

"You think of anything else, you call me, all right?" he said. "You call me right there. You seem like a nice young lady. Anything you think of might help us out, even if you don't think it will, all right?"

The office was so hot my skin felt ready to peel off. A drop of sweat was inching its way down my spine. It inched under my sports bra, slow and light as a spider's legs.

I didn't know how Officer McCarthy figured I'm a "nice young lady"—I hadn't been particularly nice that day. I'd been ornery, as my mom would say.

And I'd been lying my tail off.

You seem like a nice young lady. It just needled at me.

And just like that, I wanted to be anywhere besides that office. It didn't matter where. Just as long as it was away from Officer McCarthy, smiling at me in that too-gentle way and calling me a "nice young lady." Just as long as it was away from *here*.

That's always been the difference between Joel

and me, ever since we started the Running-Away Game this year: Joel cares about the destination, about where he's running away *to*.

I just want out.

Here's the thing: Maybe I've had a secret for a long time. Longer than Joel's been gone. Longer than this school year. Maybe I *am* a secret. But when you *are* the secret, it gets harder and harder to tell anyone. When you *are* the secret, sometimes you don't even realize it exists: If you figure you're never, ever going to tell anyone, ever, in your whole life, you can just bury that secret down like it's not there. You can keep it a secret from yourself.

Maybe.

I slid Officer McCarthy's business card into the pocket of my shorts and kept my hand there, rubbing the edges of it. I let the sharp corner bite a little into the soft part of my palm.

"Sure," I told him. "I'll let you know if I think of anything."

As we headed back to my dad's car in the parking lot, my dad wrapped his arm around my shoulders. He pulled me close in a walking one-armed hug.

"We're gonna find him," he said. "I know we are. I'm proud of you, sweet pea."

His arm around me was too tight. The ground felt like it might drop right out from under me. Kentucky gets a lot of sinkholes; most of our bedrock is limestone, and water wears through it easier than other kinds of rock. It eats it away until the limestone can't hold up the soil on top. That's what I kept picturing: Some cavern under our feet collapsing. The ground caving in. Me balanced on the edge of it, trying not to get dragged down.

He shouldn't have been proud of me. I didn't say anything at all on the drive home.

WHAT THE SEARCH PARTY FINDS

IN THE PARISH HALL AFTER THE VIGIL MASS, MARI CLARK-ESPINOZA SPOTS me and waves wildly from across the room. She and her moms didn't come to Mass. They're just here for the search. Mari's family isn't Catholic. They're the kind of folks who talk about "the universe" instead of God.

Officer McCarthy and a couple of his officers are splitting everybody up into groups. They're going to comb the woods that stretch from the church to Riverview Middle to the area behind my house—the woods where Joel disappeared. Mari tries to beckon me over to join her group, but my mom holds me back.

"We're going to stick around here for when they get back," my mom says. She leans in close so her breath tickles my ear. "I don't want you going out there."

She doesn't say what she thinks will happen if I go back to the woods. She doesn't let Teagan go, either. Instead, Teagan and me watch the groups form up and head out, and we stay there in the parish hall. Mari and her moms head outside. Rudy Thomas and his parents are joining up with a group, too. Rudy's arms are folded tight over his chest.

"I don't want to go," he's telling his mom.

Of course he doesn't. Rudy Thomas couldn't care less about finding Joel.

But he adds, "I mean, it's kind of creepy, right? Since we don't know what happened to him?"

His mom puts a hand on his shoulder to comfort him, but his dad cuts her off.

"Don't coddle him," Mr. Thomas snaps at her. Then he rounds on Rudy. "Come on. You don't see anyone else whining like a little girl."

They follow the rest of their search group out, and it's just the stragglers left, and me and my mom and

Teagan. Teagan and me get assigned to set out big boxes of doughnuts from the bakery next door, and when we're done with that, we start pots of coffee to go in the big silver dispensers. My mom and old Mrs. Fitzgerald warm up gallons of burgoo, too, left over from the church picnic last weekend. The parish hall is stuffy and warm, and the burgoo reheating on the stove makes everything smell like corn and tomato sauce. Teagan and me line up Styrofoam cups on a serving table so we can ladle out the burgoo when folks start getting back.

Maybe they'll find him, I think. *Maybe they'll walk in any minute now and Joel will be right there with them.*

But I don't really believe that.

Folks start trickling back in after an hour or so, maybe more. They report to Officer McCarthy and show him anything funny they've found, and then they file over to our table to pick out food and coffee. The first group to get back has found the campsite where Joel and me had pitched our tents that night. It was just how we'd left it.

"No signs of foul play," elderly Mr. Stiles chats as

he takes a cup of burgoo from Teagan. "So that's a good sign, right?"

The next group back has found some piles of two-by-fours and plywood near one of the forest's edges. But it's just scrap piles from the construction teams building houses in one of the new subdivisions nearby.

The third group found a few empty water bottles and a granola bar wrapper in the underbrush—but when they show it to Officer McCarthy, they all figure out that it's just litter left by a different group of searchers. Joel would never leave litter in our woods.

"One of the other groups will find something," Mrs. Peterson tells Rudy Thomas's mom while they both fill up cups of coffee. "They've got to. He can't have just disappeared."

Mrs. Thomas's eyes fall on me. "How're you doing, sweetie?" she asks me.

I don't want her to look at me. My throat feels stuck. Rudy Thomas is right behind her in line, picking out a doughnut and pretending not to notice me.

I don't say anything.

After the Thomases are out of earshot, Teagan bumps her shoulder into mine again, just like she did during Mass. Teagan's two years older than me, but I hit a growth spurt this year so we're almost the same height. We used to look almost just alike when we were younger. There are pictures of me from when I was five that could just as easily be of Teagan two years earlier.

We've grown different now, but that's not really from our physical features. It's just from who we are. Same height, but Teagan stands up straight. I started hunching my shoulders as soon as I figured out it could help hide the way my chest is growing. Same eyes, but Teagan's meet yours when she's talking to you. Mine scrape the floor and the walls and anything else to avoid making eye contact most of the time. Same thick brown hair, but Teagan wears hers in a cool bun high up on her head or in long curls over her shoulders. Mine's usually just in a scraggly ponytail right where my head meets my neck.

"You want to take a break?" Teagan asks me. "Maybe get some air? It's kind of roasting in here."

"I'm okay," I say, even though I'm not really. But getting some air won't change that.

"You sure? You seem..." She's squinting at me a

little, studying me, and I don't like it. I wish people would stop looking at me. I wish that all the time, pretty much. Another search group is filing through the parish hall doors, wiping mud off their shoes. I spot Mama Callie and Mama Elena, and then Mari, her head craning every which way.

"Oh, there's Mari," I tell Teagan, and I dodge away before she can say anything else.

Mari spots me heading her way and breaks off from the group. The adults are gathering around Officer McCarthy, updating him on whatever they found while he types out notes on a laptop. They're holding something, but I can't really see through all the people.

"Any news?" Mari asks me.

"Nothing. You?"

"Uh-uh." She pushes a piece of her hair behind one ear, but it falls right back out again. Mari's hair is cut short and wavy and pushed over to one side, with a streak of purple dye through her bangs. She has the coolest hair I've ever seen. "I mean, we took some pictures and stuff, but nothing, like, *real*. Sorry your mom kept you back."

"Yeah," I say, but I'm only half listening. Instead I'm watching the group around Officer McCarthy.

One of the searchers is holding out a dangly, mud-caked string. But the mud can't quite hide the bright purple fabric underneath, or the hook on one end.

My stomach drops. It's that sinkhole feeling again, the ground crumbling right out from under me, except this time I'm tumbling into it.

"What did your group find?" I hear my voice asking from far away.

Mari follows my gaze. She's looking at me funny. "That? Part of a stretched-out bungee cord. At least that's what Mr. Eberhart thinks. It was hooked around this big old tree over by the drainage ditch. The cord's cut, though. They don't know what it would've been hooked to."

I know that drainage ditch. It runs north to south through the whole patch of woods, slicing it in half. Years ago, Joel and me started calling that ditch Mystic Creek.

I know the tree she's talking about, too. That tree was one of the earliest ones I identified, back when I'd first started collecting field guides to learn about the different plants and animals in our woods. The tree's leaves are wavy around the edges, and it has a thick tangle of roots that poke out like fingers through the creek's muddy bank. Every summer it drops huge, hairy-looking acorns on the ground around it. A bur oak.

Underneath the mud, the bungee cord in Mr. Eberhart's hand is bright purple. Fabric on the outside, and then worn-out elastic on the inside. It hadn't been quite so stretched out when I borrowed it from my dad's bag in the garage, or when Joel and I first hooked it there. But it's been a long couple of weeks.

I know that bungee cord.

And so *I know*.

A fuzzy feeling's started in my brain and is spreading through my whole body, turning my fingers and toes tingly and numb. Automatically I start counting out all the exits from the parish hall. All the different ways I can get away. There's the main entrance, but the door's blocked by the search group still gathered around Officer McCarthy. There's the swinging side door that leads out into the parking lot. There's another door behind the tables of burgoo, through the kitchen. *I don't want to be here, I don't want to be here—*

"You know something," Mari is saying. "Don't you."

Her words are a question, but her tone isn't. I've lied by omission to Mari plenty, but lying outright is different. I can't look Mari Clark-Espinoza in the face and tell her anything but the truth.

All I do is nod.

"What is it?" Mari asks right away. "Come on, Aubrey. Do you know where he is? Do you know where to find him?"

"Sort of."

The parish hall isn't big. Nobody seems to be paying us any mind, but I can just imagine my words drifting like paper on the wind, getting picked up somewhere I don't plan. My parents are two tables away from us, eating warm, spicy burgoo from Styrofoam cups and plastic spoons. Joel's parents are just across the room. Joel's mom looks over in our direction, and I look away as fast as I can.

"Not here, okay?" I tell Mari. "I'll text you later."

"You'd better."

"I will."

Because I know what that bungee cord means. I know what had been hooked on the other end. And I know what it means if the raft is gone.

SUNDAY NIGHT

EVERYTHING ON SUNDAY AFTER THE VIGIL IS A BLUR: THE LAST OF THE search parties reporting in with Officer McCarthy, and more nice church ladies patting me on the arm, and hours of cleaning up leftover food from the parish hall. We get home in time for dinner. My mom makes us meat loaf and mashed potatoes. She and Teagan and my dad chat about the weather and my dad's vegetable garden and "*mmm*, isn't this meat loaf good." They're trying to keep things normal, I guess. To pretend, for my sake, that after this horrible day everything isn't still turned upside down. But it just makes me feel worse.

I don't talk much at dinner, and as soon as we've cleared the table, I shut myself in my room.

The little ball of wax, the one that melted off my vigil candle and onto my hand, is still smushed up in my pocket. I sit on my bed and roll it between my palms till it's round again.

I should tell my parents the truth. Joel's parents, too. I know I should. I keep thinking about Joel's mom this morning, and about her soft eyes that were hard to look at. *Do you have any idea where he might have gone?* There was something about the way she'd asked it. When Officer McCarthy was sending out the search groups, he told everyone to look out for signs of foul play—signs Joel had been kidnapped, or attacked by an animal, or had gotten hurt somehow. But Joel's mom seemed to know that wasn't it. She seemed to know that Joel had left on purpose.

Just like you wanted, I think, even though it's not like that at all.

I should call her up right now and tell her what I know about the bungee cord they found. About the raft we built.

Instead, I just keep rolling that ball of wax. A hot,

clenched-up feeling has started to roll around inside me, too.

Anger, I realize. I feel angry.

Most of the people who showed up to the vigil today have known Joel and me our whole lives. They're Joel's community. They might sit in church and pray Joel gets home safe and sing hymns about lost sheep. They might spend an hour or two looking for him in the woods.

But they're the same people who didn't do a thing to help all year. Mrs. Thomas acted like her son, Rudy, was just a class clown instead of a bully. Vice Principal McDonnell gave Rudy Thomas and Parker Ferguson "talking-tos" and then pretended not to notice when the talking-tos didn't change anything. Joel's dad rolled his eyes and acted like whatever happened was somehow Joel's fault. Joel's mom had the worst solution of all.

Grown-ups are supposed to *fix* things. They're not supposed to pretend everything's okay. They're not supposed to just let people like Rudy Thomas and his friends happen. They're not supposed to wait to see what'll happen next, to just wait till things get worse.

They've all kept saying how much they care about Joel. But it's just words.

Maybe I'm not the only one who's been telling lies.

I don't want any of them to find him. I want to—

Well. I'm still working out what I want to do.

So I do what Joel has always said I do best: I start making a plan. I pull out the stack of Post-its from my desk drawer, and I sharpen a pencil, and I start a to-do list.

Step One...

I don't sleep much that night. I lie in bed for hours. I watch the fan on my bedroom ceiling circling around, around, around, and then when I start to get dizzy I roll over and stare at my leaf collection instead. I've got a whole bulletin board of them: leaves from our woods, pressed perfectly flat and tacked up with labels from what kind of tree each leaf came from. I've written all the tree names out on index cards: *Blue Ash. Sugar Maple. Sassafras.* I like reading through the labels when I can't fall asleep. They make my brain go quiet.

I've been collecting the leaves for years. Joel and I dry them all out in the microwave and press them inside heavy books to preserve them. But some of them are still starting to go brown around the edges.

Joel was going to help me find and flatten new ones this summer.

I turn back to watching the ceiling fan instead. Joel's the only person I can talk to about leaves and plants and the names for all the things in the woods. When I start talking with other people, I can see the moment when their eyes get far away, when they get bored and stop listening. Even with Teagan. Even with my parents. I can see right when I've gotten too excited about something they don't think is worth getting excited about. I can see when they decide I'm being weird.

There was this moment back during the first week of sixth grade, when Madilyn Sellers had been asking me questions to help her finish our worksheet for plant science. We had to label which plants were vascular and which were nonvascular. I could've done it in my sleep.

"So a tree is vascular?" she'd asked.

"Yep," I said, and she marked it down.

"And moss?"

"Nonvascular. Well, except club mosses," I said. It just came out. I'd been reading up on mosses just that weekend. "But those aren't really mosses. They're misnamed. They're more like ferns than mosses, so they're vascular."

Her eyes had been getting wider and wider the more I talked. "Are we gonna have to know all that for the test?" she asked, horrified.

I told her no, that it was just interesting, and her eyes squinted up like she was confused. I knew right then I'd done something wrong. Middle school had new social rules, or at least they were new to me. It felt like everyone else had gotten a handbook except for Joel and me. That morning, I started a list in my head of Wrong Topics to Talk About:

1. Random facts about moss.

Rudy Thomas sat in front of me in that class, and

he'd turned around in his desk. He was eyeing me up and down with his mouth twisted in a little smirk.

"I think I've heard you say, like, five words since kindergarten," he said, pushing up his eyebrows in pretend shock. Laying it on thick. "*This* is what gets you talking? Some weird plant thing?"

"You're such a weirdo, Aubrey." Madilyn Sellers laughed.

The laugh wasn't mean, exactly, but it made me want to curl in on myself. The laugh, and the way she and Rudy Thomas were both looking at me. Even after she went back to asking me for worksheet answers, I stayed stuck in that moment. Seeing myself the way Madilyn Sellers did, and Rudy Thomas did—the way *other people* did.

And once I'd seen myself from the outside, it was like I couldn't stop. I hated that outside version of me that people saw—people who'd known me since kindergarten. Who thought they *knew* me. I wanted to hide, or to run away to someplace new, someplace with no one who'd ever met me before. Maybe that would fix it. If none of these people looked at me, maybe the wrong outside version of me that they saw would stop existing.

Joel wasn't in that class with me, and when we met up after the bell, I didn't tell him about any of it.

I never feel that weird, outside way around Joel. His eyes don't get far away when I get too excited about nature facts. He just gets excited right along with me. He'll search through field guides with me for hours while we try to decide if the bird we saw that afternoon was a sparrow or a whip-poor-will. He'll let me point out all the different kinds of ivy we see while we hike.

Maybe Joel understands why I get excited about my field guides because he gets excited about things, too. He gets excited about *everything*. So excited he can't hold it all at once. Joel's always jumped from one interest to the next, pulling me right along with him. You can count our whole lives just by whatever new hobby or interest Joel was into at the time. Like a couple of years ago, he got into ghost-hunting. He dragged me to places he'd decided might be haunted—the cemetery, the old high school, the

Fitzgeralds' barn—and took videos with his mom's iPad, and then he'd play them back again slow while we searched for weird sounds or orbs of light.

We hadn't found any real signs of spirits by the time he moved on to trying to make his own comic books. Then it was teaching himself to play the recorder. For a while he wanted to be a movie director, and he pulled out the iPad again. But he got bored pretty quick when he realized he couldn't both act in front of the camera *and* direct from behind it at the same time.

And then his thing for the last couple of months this year was baking. Cupcakes, mostly. He had watched some show where people baked and decorated dozens and dozens of cupcakes and then got judged against each other, and he got totally obsessed. Right away, he started printing off cupcake recipes from his dad's work computer. He checked out cupcake-decorating books from the library. He convinced his mom to take him on a special trip to Kroger so he could get flour and eggs and sugar and cocoa powder and whatever else you need to bake cupcakes.

"You know you can just buy it in a box," I told him

afterward, while we both stared across the rows of ingredients he'd lined up on the kitchen table at his house. "You can get the whole mix. Just add eggs and water and stir it up."

Joel gave me a fake-indignant look—his eyes wide and shocked, his mouth gaping open like a sideways letter *D*. I made up a name for it quick in my head: the Deeply, Personally Offended look.

"We're making them from scratch," he said.

I started to grin. "Have you ever baked anything from scratch?"

"It's about the *process*."

The process, as it turned out, was messy. The process was me reading out the recipe step-by-step, as careful as I could, while Joel skipped ahead and added too much flour and forgot the eggs and spilled cocoa powder all over the kitchen. The process that first time made twelve crusty brown blobs that were more or less shaped like cupcakes but tasted like dirt. They had a texture like chewing on a tire.

"I think we messed something up," I said after we'd both spit out our bites into the garbage can.

"I think the recipe was bad," Joel said.

But when we tried again with a different recipe the next week, they still weren't so great.

Our cupcakes slowly got better, at least a little. Our cupcake *decorations* definitely got better. It was fun either way: Measuring and bickering and both trying to make our cupcakes look better than the other's. Making a huge mess every time. Maybe we would've finally mastered it—gotten the batter all light and fluffy, cooked them just the right amount so they weren't soggy but also weren't burnt, decorated them all neat and tidy and perfect. But Joel doesn't like to stick with one thing too long. He petered out after a few months, and I followed, like I always do.

And then not long after that, we started building the raft, anyway.

THE START OF A PLAN

I MUST HAVE FALLEN ASLEEP AT SOME POINT, BUT WHEN I WAKE ON Monday morning I feel stretched out and twitchy. My brain's wound up tight, like one of those toy cars with the spinning wheels. Ever since the search party found that bungee cord, I've been pulling the wheels on the car back, back, back. I've been winding them up. Now I'm just waiting for the moment to let go and watch the car go flying.

I wait till I hear my parents bumping around the kitchen, getting ready for work, before I put my plan into action. My dad's at the kitchen table, holding half a piece of toast in one hand and reading a page of the *Bowling Green Daily News* with the other. My mom's loading up the dishwasher. On the counter beside her, the coffeepot they've had longer than I've been alive is flipped on, gurgling and spitting like an angry cat.

"Morning, sweet pea," my dad says when he sees me.

"Morning, Aubrey," my mom says. "How're you feeling?"

I've been asked that so many times in the last two days. *Jittery*, I want to say now. *Nervous. Like I want to be any other place besides here.* I don't say any of those, though. I say, "Okay, I guess," and start passing her rinsed plates from the sink without her asking.

"What're you up to today?" my dad asks me. His voice is fake cheerful, trying too hard, and it comes out muffled through the toast in his mouth. He waves the weather page of the paper at us. "Should be nice out."

"Humid, though," my mom grumbles.

It's always humid in the summer here. The air turns thick and stifling and wraps your skin up in a damp blanket. Our town of Riverview, Kentucky, is nestled in the Green River Valley, tucked in between hills and woods on either side, and all the moisture that rises off the river just gets stuck. It just stays. My mom says a Riverview summer has enough humidity to keep a fish alive in the open air.

"So?" my dad says. "What's your plan for your first day of vacation?"

Any other summer, the answer to his question would always, *always* start with the words *Joel and I*....

Here is what's on the to-do list on the Post-it note I made last night:

1. Ask my parents for permission to have a friend over.
2. Text Mari.
3. Go into the woods.
4. Find the place where the raft used to be.
5. ...

I have a few ideas about Step Five, but I haven't written those down. Writing them down would make them real, and right now they feel too fragile for that. They feel like they might crumble away at the littlest touch.

I stick with Step One.

"Can I have a friend over?" I ask.

My mom drops another plate into the dishwasher. It rattles a little bit when it lands. She wipes her wet hands on her pants.

"Who?" she asks.

"Just Mari," I say.

"Are her...parents...okay with Teagan being in charge?" she asks. She says the word *parents* carefully. She never pauses like that when she's talking about Joel's mom and dad. Or *anybody's* mom and dad. Just Mari's parents, since both her parents are moms.

"I'll check," I say.

"And is Teagan okay with being in charge of both of you?"

"I'll check that, too."

She's about to ask more questions. Another time, she'd probably ask what we were going to do together, or if Mari was planning to stay for lunch. She might ask to talk to Mari's moms herself. She might ask the kinds of questions that would mean I couldn't just lie by omission. I'd have to lie outright.

But I know this part of their morning routine, and I've timed it just right. Before she can get to any more questions, the coffeepot beeps that it's ready, and my dad spots the clock on the microwave and says, "Shoot, running late," and my mom says, "Do you have your keys?" and then he and my mom are both a flurry of pouring coffee and closing the dishwasher and finding my dad's car keys buried under the stack of newspaper sections.

"Have fun with Mari," my mom says as she hurries out the door. She presses a kiss into my hair, just over my forehead.

My dad's already turned on the car. It's rumbling in the garage.

At the last minute, my mom turns back to me. "And stay out of the woods, okay?" she says.

"I will," I say.

Fine, so I lied outright after all.

I send Mari a text:

Ok we can talk

She calls instead of texting back. I guess I'm not surprised. Mari always says she likes talking better than texting, and anyway, she says I text too slow. I'm the last person in the universe to get a smartphone, so I still have to punch out all the letters one by one with the nine number keys. My parents only let Teagan get a smartphone this year. My mom says I'm still too young, and I "don't need to spend every minute on all that" yet.

"Finally," Mari says when I answer. "What's going on? Where is he? What's the plan?"

"The plan is still coming together," I say. She's jumped straight in like she always does, without even saying hello. I take a deep breath.

"Can you come over?" I say.

"Of course," she says. No hesitation. I don't know why, but I was at least expecting her to hesitate. We've been friends all year, and I still keep expecting her to make up reasons not to be around me. "Now? I'm coming now. I'll get Mama Elena to drive. Should I bring anything?"

"Comfortable shoes," I say.

"Of course," she says again.

"We're going to the woods."

I try to say it like it's no big deal. But my voice shakes on the word *woods*. I've been clutching my phone tighter and tighter in my hand, so tight my fingers are starting to sweat.

The woods are my and Joel's spot.

Were our spot.

No. *Are* our spot.

Anyway, Mari knows it's a big deal for me.

Mari's quiet for a few seconds. Then she just says, "Okay. See you in ten minutes," and hangs up.

MAMA ELENA

MARI'S FAMILY JUST MOVED TO RIVERVIEW THIS YEAR, WHICH IS UNUSUAL, because most people don't *move to* Riverview. Most people in Riverview have just always been in Riverview. One of Mari's moms, Mama Callie, grew up in Riverview and lived here ages and ages ago; she and Mama Elena and Mari moved back to take care of Mari's grandmother. So I get why they're here. But still—it's unusual for somebody who left Riverview to come *back*.

I hear their car pull in, and by the time I tug on my old sneakers and sprint outside, Mari's marching up the driveway with Mama Elena right behind her. Their hair is the exact same color, glossy black that shines penny brown in sunlight. But Mama Elena's is pulled back in a long, high ponytail. Mari's is loose and spiky, and her purple-streaked bangs are already damp with sweat.

"Hi, Aubrey," Mama Elena says. "Is it just you today?"

"My sister's here, too," I say.

Mari's moms have told Joel and me over and over again to call them "Mama Elena" and "Mama Callie." Like they're our own mamas. But it still feels weird to me. Mari says it's less confusing for her than calling them both Mom, or having me call them both Mrs. Clark-Espinoza.

"What are you two planning this morning?" Mama Elena asks.

"Nothing much," I say.

"Just hanging out," Mari says.

I figure Mama Elena might ask to talk to Teagan— my mom would definitely ask to talk to whoever was in charge. But instead she just drills Mari on a couple of emergency numbers, and then tells us to call her if we need anything, and then reminds Mari to behave herself.

"And you'll call me if you need me?" Mama Elena asks her one last time. "If you—"

"*Mo-o-om*," Mari cuts her off, darting her eyes over to me and away just as quick. I can tell she's embarrassed by whatever her mom was going to say, but I don't ask. "I'm good. We're good."

Before she gets back in the car, though, Mama Elena rests one hand on my shoulder, very lightly. She looks me straight in the eyes.

"I hope you're doing okay," Mama Elena says. She doesn't make it a question. She doesn't make me say whether I'm doing okay or not. "Let me know if there's anything you need, all right? Anything at all."

People have been saying stuff like this to me for days. My parents, and Officer McCarthy, and lots of people from church. But when Mama Elena says it, she sounds more sincere than most people. Like she actually means it. That makes me wonder if anyone else actually has, or if it's just more empty words and lies.

"Thanks," I say. My voice sounds flat, like I'm reading from a script. I force a Cover-Up Smile. Just like the one Joel makes when he's pretending everything's fine. "I think it'll be good to take my mind off everything that's happened for a while."

Mari and I are not taking our minds off it, though. We're doing the opposite. As soon as Mama Elena pulls her car back into the street, Mari grins at me. We don't even go through the house, which is good— we don't have to worry about running into Teagan. Instead, we duck through the side yard and around to the back.

And then we take off into the woods.

FAIRY RAFTS

THE FIRST TIME WE ACTUALLY RAN AWAY FROM SCHOOL, IT WAS JOEL'S idea. We had two more weeks left of sixth grade at that point. Summer vacation was staring us down, just out of reach. We'd been playing the Running-Away Game all year, making up wild plans to escape from Riverview. But we were never going to actually *do* them. We just played the game, talked the plan through, and then went to our next class. We let the game stay a game.

But that afternoon was different. After Joel convinced me to leave, we used an escape route I'd mapped out in my head ages before. We climbed over the chain-link fence by the science annex and ran across the back football fields. Once we'd reached the woods, we both doubled over to catch our breath, grinning at each other. I could barely believe we'd really done it.

The patch of woods behind the school spreads right through the heart of Riverview. It stretches from the football fields behind Riverview Middle School on one side, to the neighborhood where Joel and I live on another side, to the back of the Church of the Sacred Heart on another side, to the new strip mall with the hair salon and the burrito bar on *another* side. The woods connect all these different parts of Riverview, but when you're inside them, they feel like they're totally separate. They don't feel connected to anything at all.

We started walking. Just hiking along the trails, just like we always do. I pointed out the pincushion moss climbing up a tree branch, and a big patch of Virginia creeper. My hands were shaking a little, and my heartbeat still hadn't slowed down. But it was good jitters.

We'd been hiking for a while when we heard Mystic

Creek. Mystic Creek runs straight through the middle of our patch of woods. Pretty nearly every trail leads to it eventually. By the time it came into view, I'd even stopped worrying about whether Mr. Calhoun in our seventh-period history class had noticed we were gone and whether he'd call our parents. Riverview Middle felt far away. It felt like a different world, and the world in the woods felt a lot more real.

"Want to build fairy rafts?" Joel asked when we'd reached the banks of the creek.

We used to build fairy rafts all the time. Back in elementary school, we'd spend recess picking out a handful of twigs all the same width from the playground. Then we'd pull long strands of ryegrass from over by the fence, where nobody ever mowed, and we'd weave it in and out of the twigs and make flat little raft beds. Fairy-sized rafts. Sometimes, Joel and me would float them in the puddle that always formed at the bottom of the playground slide when it rained.

We hadn't built fairy rafts at all this year. Riverview Middle doesn't have recess; it has PE, where you have to play organized sports and deal with Rudy Thomas.

Joel was already starting to hunt for fairy raft materials on the ground. So I said, "Sure," and we picked out sticks and grass and sat down there on the muddy bank and strung them all together. I kept weaving mine too tight and making the twigs fall apart. But Joel's worked. He peeled off his sneakers and slid barefoot down the side of the ditch till he was standing in the shin-deep water of Mystic Creek.

"Moment of truth," he announced, and he did a dramatic flourish before he plopped the raft in the water.

It floated perfectly.

He let it bounce back and forth between his hands, trapped, till I finally gave up on my raft and scrambled down into the creek to join him. The water was icy. I curled my toes in the sandy mud on the bottom, layered over the concrete, and I waited for my feet to go numb enough that I wouldn't feel the cold anymore.

When I looked up at Joel, he was smirking at me.

"Looks like somebody's out of practice at making fairy rafts."

"Shut up," I said.

"Guess I'm the captain this time. You can be my first mate, if you want. Good experience with following orders and swabbing the—Hey!"

I'd grabbed the boat right out of his hands. "And the first mate commandeers your vessel!"

Joel called it a mutiny, and we fought over that little bundle of sticks and grass till we were both splattered with mud and water. By the time we climbed back up out of the creek, Joel looked like he'd spent the afternoon at a pig farm. We wiped our muddy hands on our shorts and pulled on our sneakers.

That's when the cold settled back in. All of a sudden I felt guilty. Guilty for being so immature. For goofing around like little kids. Joel and me are supposed to be middle schoolers now.

I miss elementary school. Before the Rudy Thomas problem started. Before Joel's dad got worse. Before Joel had mastered the Cover-Up Smile.

In the end, even though I knew it was silly, we dropped what was left of Joel's fairy raft back down into the creek and watched till it was out of sight. Joel asked me where I thought the creek went, and I told him the real answer, but in my mind I didn't quite believe it. In my mind, the raft would round the bend into the trees up ahead and just be gone. Disappeared from view and existence.

INTO THE WOODS

THE WOODS ARE QUIET AS MARI AND I WALK. EVEN WHEN I'M CROSSING them with Joel, the woods are quiet—and Joel is about as quiet as a bag of marbles in a tumble dryer. The big curving trees muffle out the rest of the world. They filter the sunlight through their branches and make everything soft and glowing.

Mari and I pass all the usual landmarks Joel and I have named for our different games. Here's the Sacred Spot, the clearing where we hold ceremonies when we play our Woodland Elves game. That rocky bluff overlooking the strip mall used to be Pride Rock, back when we would pretend we were Disney lions. We could survey our kingdom from the top of it. This murky pond covered in algae is sometimes one of the seven seas or sometimes the canoe lake at Camp Half-Blood, depending on whether we're playing Pirates or Percy Jackson that day.

Most of the time when Joel and I are here, we're playing our games—we're pretending to be somebody else. It's funny how that's maybe the only time I stop watching myself from the outside these days. The only time I can just exist on the inside and actually feel like *me*.

Since we're coming from the direction of Joel's and my house, we find the campsite first. A ring of big, jagged rocks makes a fire circle in the middle of the clearing. Its center is dark and charred from the fire Joel and I had here just a couple of nights ago. Around the fire circle are two sets of holes in the dirt from where we staked down the tents.

This was the first year Joel and I camped in *tents*, plural. Two of them. Every year before now, we just used one tent, and that was fine, and no one questioned it. But this year that stopped being okay, I guess. This year, Joel's parents and my parents talked to each other when Joel and I weren't there. They all decided that having two tents would be more "appropriate."

"You two are getting too old for sleepovers," Joel's dad had told us. It was a week before our camping trip. He and my dad and my mom had sat the both of us down in the Gallaghers' living room, on the vinyl sofa that always makes my legs sweat. "You're not little kids anymore."

I looked at my mom and dad, who hadn't said a word. "Teagan still has sleepovers," I pointed out.

"Your sister has sleepovers with *other girls*," my dad said. He kept cutting his eyes over to my mom, picking out his words carefully. "It's different. Joel's a boy, and you're a girl."

I didn't know why that made anger flash through me, hot like lightning. I didn't know why I hated, hated, hated my dad for pointing that out.

"We have to have some different rules for that," he said.

The angry heat in me felt itchy, prickling in my chest and the backs of my legs and the inside of my skull. The sofa fabric was sticking to my thighs. I

74

looked at my knees because I didn't want to look at any of them right then. My knees were pinkish and scratched-up and had prickly dark hairs growing on them. Before this year, nobody cared about who shaved their legs and who didn't. But it turns out it's one of the new middle school rules. If you're a girl, shaving your legs is the normal thing. *Not* shaving your legs is wrong.

Why do the rules have to be different? I wanted to demand.

If we're not little kids anymore, then what are we? Teenagers? I didn't feel like a teenager.

Mostly, though, I just kept thinking, *I don't want to be here.* That room and the sticky sofa and our parents' eyes on us made me feel outside myself and wrong. I felt far away already—like my heart had taken off running somewhere, and the rest of me was itching to go with it.

Joel was sitting right beside me on the couch. I thought he might say something even if I couldn't. I don't usually say much, but Joel does. And he had to be thinking all the same thoughts I was.

Maybe he would've spoken up if his mom was

there. But she was still at work at the hospital. Instead, he just nodded at his dad and said, "Yes, sir."

Afterward, Joel and I went back to the woods to keep working on our raft before the sun set all the way. We were finishing the frame at that point. We hammered the big plywood sheets onto the two-by-fours we'd screwed together. My hot anger had passed, but I still felt on edge.

"I don't know why they're making such a big deal, with the two tents thing," I said.

Joel didn't answer. He just kept hammering. *Bap-bap-bap.*

"We've camped out like a million times before," I said.

Joel finished knocking in the nail on the corner of the raft and passed the hammer to me. He sat back in the dirt and picked up a crooked stick off the ground, rattling it back and forth along the bur oak tree's rough bark.

"I mean, what do they think we're going to *do*?" I asked.

"This one'd be a good sword," Joel said suddenly, like he hadn't heard a word I'd said. He held his stick in front of him and stabbed it around a little as a test. "Curved, like a scimitar. Hey, do you want to play Pirates? Are we still on the part where we're fighting the Armies of the Dead?"

The Armies of the Dead is this fleet of ghost pirate ships that Joel had added into our Pirates game. We tucked our tools under the raft for the next day. I picked out a stick for a sword, too, and we decided on our characters for the afternoon: Joel was a prince fleeing from his wicked uncle, who was vying for the throne. I was Captain William Hawk, who'd run away as a child to pursue a life of piracy and saved up to buy his own ship. We practiced with our stick swords and played out our story, and the whole time, a prickly little voice in my head kept saying, *We're too old for this.*

I didn't want to think it. I don't want to be too old for our games in the woods.

But it was like as soon as my parents had said that the rules for Joel and me were different now, I couldn't stop thinking it. I wanted to become Captain Hawk without seeing the wrong outside version of me at the same time: this scraggly-ponytailed girl who has to wear sports bras and doesn't know how to shave her legs.

I didn't want to have to hear my dad's voice in my head saying, *Joel's a boy, and you're a girl.* Telling us that we're not little kids anymore. Telling us that everything's changing.

All the changes feel like they're happening to the wrong person.

Now, on Monday, as Mari and I hike wordlessly through the woods, I keep thinking about the night of Joel's and my camping trip. I keep remembering what *did* happen when we tried to camp out in our two tents. The thing that happened before we fought. Had Joel already planned that before our parents sat us down to tell us we had to have separate tents? Or did he decide after? Maybe that conversation planted the idea. Maybe that conversation caused our fight.

All of a sudden this place feels like it's all just a little bit wrong. Or maybe *I'm* just wrong. The same itchy, prickly feeling I had on the couch that day has come back. I start walking faster. Mari's feet kick along behind me quicker to keep up. She trips on a root and stumbles forward.

"Hey, wait up a sec," Mari says.

Mari doesn't shave her legs, either. I don't know why this is the piece I get stuck on. Mari's legs are covered in soft dark hairs. "Women only started shaving their legs after razor companies told them to," she said one day, after Madilyn Sellers had pointed out Mari's leg hair in social studies class. "And the razor companies only said that because they wanted to sell more razors."

"I just feel like it's unhygienic," Madilyn had said, wrinkling her nose.

"No, it's *capitalism*," Mari said. "Besides, no one calls it unhygienic when *guys* don't shave their legs."

I'd tugged on the cuffs of my jeans under my desk, suddenly glad I'd worn pants instead of shorts that day. But Mari didn't seem to care when the other girls in our class whispered about her. She never does.

That makes the itchy feeling fade a little. Even when I've felt like *I* was doing something wrong for not wanting to shave my legs, I've never thought that about Mari.

I slow down my walking a little bit and let Mari catch up with me. And then we can hear Mystic Creek.

ON THE BANKS OF MYSTIC CREEK

THE OLD BUR OAK TREE LEANS OUT OVER MYSTIC CREEK, JUST LIKE IT always has. Mystic Creek isn't really a creek, though. It's barely even a stream. Really, it's a drainage ditch, about twice my height across, with a cracked layer of concrete lining its bottom. It doesn't have a real name, and Joel and I named it Mystic Creek so long ago that I don't even remember where the name came from. Maybe it was part of a game. Maybe we just liked how it sounded.

"This is where we found the bungee yesterday," Mari says now, nodding at the tree. "You know what it was attached to?"

My voice feels clogged. I've spent too many days not saying things, and the things I haven't said have piled up.

I picture the bungee cord when we first hooked it here: one end looped around the tree's trunk, the other hooked to the raft. We'd done it to keep the raft from getting swept away without us if Mystic Creek overflowed. After Mari's search group brought the cut bungee back to the parish hall, I'd wondered why Joel had cut the whole cord in half instead of just unhooking it.

But now that I'm standing here, in the spot where he must've come after we split up that night, I can see the whole scene. It plays out in my mind so clear it feels real. I can see Joel's stretched-out collar of his old T-shirt, the way the humidity that night made his hair curlier than ever. I can see Joel climbing aboard the raft. Joel using his foot, or maybe the oar we'd made, or maybe both to push the whole thing—the raft, his backpack, and himself—off the bank and out into the current of Mystic Creek.

Right away, the water tries to tug the raft further

in. It strains on the bungee, pulls it too tight to unhook. Joel takes out his pocketknife, the one his dad gave him for his twelfth birthday. He'd told Joel the knife would help him in the woods, but he'd either forgotten or was pretending not to know that most of what Joel does in the woods doesn't need a real knife. His dad is always trying to toughen him up. But you don't need a pocketknife to play our pretend games or collect leaves or listen to birdcalls. Before this night, I don't know if Joel had ever even used it.

He uses it now, though. I know he does. I can see him sawing through the bungee, the only thing holding him and the raft back. I can feel the imaginary string between us, stretching from him to me.

The elastic snaps. And just like that, he's off, he's off, he's *off.*

I can see it all so clearly. It worked. The raft must have worked.

Because Joel isn't here.

Mari is still watching me, waiting for an answer. I swallow.

"A raft," I say, and just like that, my voice comes

unstuck. It's like imagining Joel and the raft getting swept downriver made my voice get swept right out of me. "It was hooked to a raft."

Mari's eyes are wide. "Where'd you get a raft?" she says.

"We built it," I say.

"This is where you and Joel kept disappearing to?" she says. "When you kept sneaking out of school?"

"Yeah," I say.

"What did you build the raft out of?"

"Wood. From where they're building new houses. The scrap piles at the construction sites. And we rolled a couple of blue plastic trash barrels from behind the school to make it float."

"And it floated? It worked, I mean?"

"It worked good enough."

"And now the raft is . . . ?"

She's putting the puzzle pieces together. I can practically see her mind turning. She squats down at the base of the tree and rests her chin on her knees. I breathe in, slow. I breathe out, slower. It feels like I haven't taken a deep breath since Friday.

I pick up a stick the length of my forearm and snap off a few pieces—*snap, snap, snap*—and toss them in the water. They bob in the current and drift downstream until they round the bend and disappear out of sight.

THE PICTURE ON OFFICER McCARTHY'S DESK

AT THE POLICE STATION, WHEN I WAS TALKING TO OFFICER McCARTHY, HE kept Joel's school picture pointing at us on the table. I'd seen that photo a million times before on the wall at Joel's house. But I'd only ever seen it while Joel— the *real* Joel—was standing right beside me. So I'd never noticed it before.

But here's the thing: Joel never really looks like himself in still photographs, because in real life, Joel Gallagher is always, *always* in motion. Looking at a still photo of Joel when he's not there beside you, bouncing around the room and talking nonstop about whatever new interest he's been into lately and using goofy voices and being alive—it feels like he's gone. *Really* gone. It feels like the picture's just a thing, and Joel doesn't exist anymore.

The whole time I was answering Officer McCarthy's questions, I stared at that photo. It made my stomach feel hollowed out. The questions he asked me only covered Joel's last couple of weeks. But my brain kept feeding me older memories: Joel and me flipping through my field guides to find blue sage and milkweed and goldenrod, picking them and mashing them up in an empty yogurt cup to use in our magic elvish healing potion. Joel and me racing each other along the trail to Mystic Creek. Joel and me climbing the huge rock in the woods that we always use as our ship during our Pirates game, fighting over who's going to play as the captain that day—but the kind of fight that ends with us laughing so hard we fall over.

And then I was thinking about the other fight we had—the real one. And about what happened on the last day of school. And the things Vice Principal McDonnell said. And about how much I'd been seeing the Cover-Up Smile on Joel's face this year, distant and not quite real and plastering over something worse.

And Officer McCarthy had kept saying Joel would turn up, that we didn't have anything to worry about, but if you ask me, we should've been worrying already. We should've been worrying for a long time, long before Joel disappeared. Because even before he disappeared, he hadn't been okay. And no one had done anything.

And I didn't do anything, either.

That's a piece that's hard to confess, but I'm confessing it anyway. I got so worried about Joel maybe leaving me that I forgot all about why he'd *want* to leave. I didn't do enough.

WHERE THE CREEK GOES

I'M BENDING DOWN TO PICK UP ANOTHER STICK WHEN I NOTICE IT.

Back in third grade, Joel and me learned from one of my library books how to make nature-friendly trail markers so hikers don't get lost. We didn't really need the markers to navigate our woods. We already knew all the trails here. But we turned the trail markers into part of our Woodland Elves game. Whenever the two of us split up, one of us would leave markers to guide the other back to a rendezvous spot.

At a fork in the trail, we'd arrange sticks on the ground into an arrow shape to show which path to take. Or sometimes we'd make a big stack of stones, high enough to spot from a little ways off, to signal that you were on the right track.

I stare down at the sticks by my feet. It's not the kind of thing the search party would've noticed. To anyone besides Joel and me, it's just sticks on the ground. They're muddy and a little crooked, and maybe they're just a coincidence. Not a sign.

But the longer I stare, the more sure I am.

The sticks make an arrow. It's pointing downriver.

"I think...," I start, but I'm not ready to say it.

Mari is still squatting by the water's edge. She's pretending very hard that she isn't watching me, but I'm almost sure she's watching me.

"I think he wants..."

I think he wants us to follow him.

But I can't say it. Why do I think I have any idea what Joel wants? We used to talk about everything, Joel and me. But this year we've been leaving more and more pieces out. Things that are hard or scary to talk about. Maybe I don't know what Joel wants anymore.

Because clearly, what Joel wanted was to leave.

"You okay?" Mari asks me.

I just nod. I don't tell her about the stick arrow under my feet.

She pushes herself up. "What do we do now?" she asks.

The water pulls dirt and twigs and grass and pebbles along the creek bed. The current sounds like it's whispering: *rush, rush, rush.* How fast is the water moving? How fast was it moving on Friday night, when Joel came here after our camping trip? How fast could the creek possibly carry him away?

Beyond our smaller patch of woods, Mystic Creek drains into the Green River. We studied the Green River back in elementary school. The river is narrow, and it's steady, and it's miles long: It stretches diagonal across half the state before it empties into the bigger Ohio River. But it doesn't take a straight route there. It zigs and zags more times than a bumblebee. It winds and twists and bends its way through the heart of Kentucky.

I can feel my brain prickling with new pieces of a plan. Joel's been traveling for two days already. But he's only been traveling on the river, which means he's been going in a zigzag.

I take another stick from the ground. Not one that's making up the arrow. This one's bigger, with damp bark that comes away dark and gritty in my palm. My hands are feeling slick and shaky, so I pass the stick to Mari.

"Here, toss this in the water," I say.

She doesn't question it. Just pulls back and hurls the stick out into the middle of the creek. It disappears for a second before it bobs back to the surface and starts drifting along. It's showing us the speed of the current.

I start walking alongside it, slow at first. Almost painfully slow. Trying to match the water's pace. But Mari falls into step beside me, and she's walking faster. As soon as we start walking at a normal speed, we pass the stick.

Mystic Creek is noisy. It *sounds* like it's whispering *rush, rush, rush*. But truth be told, it travels pretty slow. Mari and I can outpace it just on foot.

I don't know if Joel really made that arrow out of sticks for me, asking me to follow him. But I've known what Step Five of my plan is all along. Since the search party brought the muddy bungee cord back to church. Maybe even since I first realized Joel was gone. I've known what I need to do, but I've been afraid to say it.

The woods today smell like fresh grass and dampness and sweet early-summer breezes. It's a familiar smell, and also a freeing one.

"I'm going after him," I say.

I say it to the creek and the water and the woods all around me. I say it to the air. I say it to myself.

And I say it to Mari, too, I guess, because from behind me, Mari says right away, "I'm coming with you."

No hesitation. No question in her voice.

"We'll find him," she says. "He needs us, right? He needs somebody watching out for him."

"Yeah," I say. "He does."

The plan's coming together now, all in a rush. Mari and I talk it through. We'll take a more direct route. We won't follow the bends and turns of the river, at least not until we're getting close to Joel. We'll look at the maps, follow a straighter path. We'll catch the river on just enough of its zigs and zags to check if there's any sign of Joel. He has a head start, but we can walk faster than the water's moving. We can catch up.

I can wish all I want that I noticed Joel needed help before he left. But it doesn't change anything. It's too late to fix what's already happened. Confessing doesn't take it away.

But I can make it right. If anyone is going to find Joel, it's not going to be Officer McCarthy or a search party. It's not going to be any of the people in town who say one thing, say they care about Joel, and then don't do anything about it. The people who've been lying just as much as me.

It's going to be me.

Mari is brushing her dirty hands off on her shorts. "Okay," she says. "Let's grab supplies. Let's figure out the route." She looks down the length of the creek. The trees in this section of the woods are spread out enough that the morning sun can shine on the water's surface in some places—so glittering and bright it hurts to look at. "Where does this go, anyway?" she asks.

Joel had asked the same question on that first afternoon when we snuck out of school and built the fairy rafts. Two weeks before the end of sixth grade. That afternoon, Joel had gazed down this length of Mystic Creek and asked me, "Where do you think this goes?"

"The Green River," I'd said then. Every source of water around Riverview flows into the Green, one way or another. "And then the Green leads to the Ohio, which leads to the Mississippi, which leads to the Gulf of Mexico."

That's the technical answer. It's the answer I give Mari now as we keep talking through our plan. But it's not the answer that really matters—not to me, anyway.

The real answer is different. It's the piece inside me that pushed us to start the Running-Away Game, even when I knew I would never *actually* run away. It's what makes me plan out escape routes from every classroom in Riverview Middle School. It's what makes me want to crawl out of my skin sometimes, and what makes me fantasize about just disappearing from Riverview—a miracle, *poof*, because sometimes I don't want to be me, and I can't explain why, and it feels easier to just be someone else, some*place* else, than to have to keep being me, here.

Maybe it's tied to the piece of me that's a secret. Because I think there's something wrong with me, that *I'm* wrong, and maybe I'd rather just hide away completely than have to admit what it is.

Joel cared about where the creek ends up. But for me, the only thing that really matters about where the creek goes is this:

It goes *away*.

PART TWO

ONE REASON JOEL LEFT

JOEL ALWAYS SAYS I MAKE TOO MANY LISTS. HE SAYS THAT SOME THINGS shouldn't get numbered off, just like that. Some things are more complicated. But it helps, I think, to line the reasons up. It helps to fit them all together so they make an answer, so everything makes sense. I'm trying to put together the pieces—to figure out all the reasons Joel ran away.

Here is one piece I figure is at the top of the list of why Joel left: Joel's dad.

Joel and me have always done most of our playing pretend in the woods, but not all of it. We used to use my dad's garden as the strawberry fields of Camp Half-Blood. We used Joel's bedroom as the captain's cabin on the ship for our Pirates game, and we used the dark spot under Joel's back porch as the interrogation room for Secret Agents.

But for the last year, we've *only* played in the woods. About a year ago, back in fifth grade, we were playing in Joel's backyard, and he'd just watched a bunch of episodes of some new show called *She-Ra and the Princesses of Power* that he'd found online. Joel watches all kinds of TV shows that I've never seen. My mom is super strict about what I can read and watch online, and I'm only allowed to use the laptop out in the family room. Joel's parents let him watch whatever he wants, mostly. They're only strict about other stuff.

Joel was convinced that *She-Ra* would make a great game for us to play. "She transforms into this super-tall princess," he'd said, "and she fights with a bunch of other princesses who all have different powers. You can be She-Ra, since you're a girl."

I'd made a face. "Let's play something else." Just thinking about it made me feel weird and far away.

Outside myself again. The most fun part of our pretend games is getting to be somebody else. I didn't see the point if I had to play as a princess just because I was a girl—if I was playing as somebody I didn't *want* to be.

"Or you can be one of the other princesses if you want!" Joel had said. "There's Glimmer, who can teleport, or Mermista, who's got water powers—"

"I don't want to be a princess," I cut in.

"I mean, they're not *princesses* like you're thinking. They're warriors! They're super powerful, and She-Ra has this magic sword she can transform into all kinds of stuff, and she's goofy and brave and—"

"Why don't *you* play as She-Ra, then?" I'd said.

So he did, and I fought alongside him as just a regular warrior, not a princess, and it turned out the game was actually pretty fun. It had sword-fighting and robots and lots of scenes of us dramatically saving villagers from the Evil Horde.

Except that after we'd been playing for a while, I noticed that Joel's dad had come out onto the back porch of their house and was watching us play.

I didn't know how long he'd been there. I didn't know how much he'd heard.

Joel's dad has always scared me a little. He's super tall, so tall he looms over you. So tall you have to crane your neck up to look at his face. And he doesn't smile very much. And a couple of times, I've heard Joel's dad yell. When my parents get upset, their voices might get frustrated or disappointed. But they never actually *yell*.

He's like the exact opposite of Joel's mom, who's usually smiling and bubbly. This year, he and Joel's mom have started fighting more and more. Joel's told me when it happens, but when I ask if he wants to talk about it, he'll always just say, "What's there to talk about?"

Joel and his dad don't look much alike. Joel's dad's face is peachy pink instead of brown. His eyes are small and close together and always look tired. Instead of Joel's dark curls, his dad's hair is light and fine as duck fluff.

But every once in a while, Joel and his dad will make a face that's just the same. That day, the face Joel's dad was making on the porch wasn't a familiar one. It wasn't a face Joel had ever really made before sixth grade. That afternoon, the ends of Joel's dad's mouth curved down, and a little wrinkle pressed into the skin between his eyebrows, and his eyes turned distant, like they'd ducked behind an invisible wall.

It's only now, when I'm putting the pieces together and remembering that face, that it feels familiar. It's the face Joel was making the last time I saw him. After we fought. Right before he left.

"You need to come in for dinner," Joel's dad told Joel then.

The way he said it, I knew there was more to it. It wasn't just that the casserole or the tacos or whatever the Gallaghers were eating that night was ready. Joel stiffened.

"I'll be in in a minute," Joel said. He'd snapped right back out of the voice he'd been using to play She-Ra, which was wild and excited and free. Now he sounded like a robot.

"Not in a minute," Joel's dad said. "Right. Now." He honed in on me, and I felt myself flinch. "You need to go home."

"Can Aubrey stay for dinner?" Joel asked.

"Not tonight."

His dad's face, I realized, held anger—a simmering anger, a slow burn. Joel muttered a "See you tomorrow" to me and walked inside, slow. I walked home. The whole time I walked, I kept seeing his dad's face. And then the face from that day got tangled up with his dad's face at other times: after Joel told him that he didn't want to play baseball anymore, and after he found out Joel had quit the Cub Scouts, and another time, years ago, when he'd walked in on Joel and me making our Woodland Elves costumes in Joel's basement. I'd found a pair of worn leather boots, four sizes too big, and turned an old T-shirt into a tunic. Joel had a flowing shawl draped over his shoulders, a delicate crown made from one of his mom's necklaces circling his head.

"Get that stuff off," Joel's dad had snapped then. Except he hadn't said "stuff." That was the first time I'd heard a grown-up swear.

The morning after Joel's dad found us playing She-Ra, Joel and I met up at school together like usual. I asked him if he wanted to play She-Ra again that day after school let out. Joel just shook his head and changed the subject.

After that, we only played our games in the woods. We only played our games where it was just the two of us.

A NEW LIST

AFTER WE FIND JOEL'S TRAIL MARKER, I ALMOST WANT TO SET OFF AFTER him right away, without even stopping back at my house. Almost. But we need supplies. We need a plan. That's the difference between Joel and me: I always need a plan.

I start making a new list in my head as Mari and I hike back to my house. Everything looks brighter when I know what's coming next. Everything looks better when you can lay out steps that'll lead to an answer.

Here is our new plan:

Step One: Sneak back into the house without

letting Teagan know we're there. This is key. If she knows, she'll start asking questions, and she'll probably tell our parents, and Mari and I will get grounded before we even leave.

Step Two: Pack up my backpack. Things we'll need: snacks, peanut butter sandwiches, water bottles, flashlights, a compass, a first aid kit. Probably some of my field guides, too, if I can fit them inside.

Step Three: Download maps of the area onto Mari's phone. She has a smartphone, one with a good GPS that can guide us through the woods. We test it out now as we walk. There's a little blue dot on the map showing where we are, and it moves toward my house as we do. Once we set out, we'll follow that more or less in the direction of the river, checking in along the banks every so often to look for signs of Joel.

Step Four: Find Joel and bring him back.

Mari is still mostly quiet once we've confirmed that the GPS will work. She pads along the path behind me, focused.

Mari had started sitting at a lunch table with Joel and me a month or two into the school year. Before that, she ate with the girls' soccer team, or sometimes with a group of kids from our social studies class. But then one day, there she was. Joel and me got through the lunch line with our trays of watery spaghetti and found Mari already eating at the table at the far-left end of the cafeteria—the one Joel and me had been sitting at every single day.

Maybe she doesn't know that's our table, I had thought.

But when she spotted us heading her way, she gave a little wave. Her mouth twisted over into this crooked smile that made her eyes squint up.

"Hi," Mari said when we reached the table. "Is it cool if I—?"

But the *sit with you?* at the end of her sentence got cut off by Joel calling out, "Mariiiii!" like she wasn't three feet away from us. He gave her a high five. Joel has this way of saying your name, pulling it out long through a grin, that makes it feel like there's nobody else in the world he'd rather be seeing right then. I've heard him say *Aubreeeey!* in that same voice practically every day since kindergarten.

"Of course it's cool," Joel said. He plonked his tray

down across the table from her. I sat down beside him, slower. "How're you?"

"Hmm," Mari said. "So-so." Something about how she said it meant there was a story there, but I didn't know how to ask what had happened, so I didn't. She wasn't eating the school spaghetti; she'd packed her lunch in Tupperware containers in a blue zippered bag with polka dots on it.

"What's that?" Joel asked, nodding at one of her Tupperwares. It was filled with little greenish beans.

"Edamame."

Joel took one without asking and popped it in his mouth. I cringed.

"Sorry," I told Mari. "Usually he only steals *my* food."

But Mari was laughing. "Happy to share," she said.

Joel swallowed his edamame and went back in for another one. "Okay, these are *really* good. Hey, you're joining drama, right? Did you hear we might be doing *The Lion, the Witch and the Wardrobe* in the spring?" He tipped his head sideways at Mari. "You act, right?"

"Yeah, sometimes," Mari said.

"You should join drama, too, Aubrey." He kicked me under the table. When I didn't answer, he kicked me again, harder. "You should act! You're really good."

"Absolutely not," I said.

"Have you been in plays before?" Mari asked me.

Joel answered for me. "Not onstage. She's *great* when we're playing, though. Like when you're being the pirate captain? You just, like, completely transform."

This time, *I* kicked *him*. He wasn't supposed to talk about our games at school. But Mari just tipped her edamame box toward me, offering it, and I took one.

Joel was right. It was really good.

We settled in like that, talking and eating and sharing edamame, like it was totally normal for Mari to sit at our lunch table. We talked some more about the spring play. We complained some about Mrs. Littlewood, our social studies teacher, who even this far into the school year was still calling Mari "Mary," no matter how many times Mari had corrected her. *Rhymes with "sorry,"* Mari said every time.

"Your name's so cool, though," Joel said, tracing his fork back and forth through his spaghetti. His other hand was drumming out a rhythm on the table. "People are the worst."

"It's short for Mariposa," Mari said, wrinkling up her nose a little bit.

"What's wrong with Mariposa?" Joel asked.

"It's the Spanish word for 'butterfly.'"

Joel just kept looking at her blankly. "What's wrong with butterflies?" he said.

"Nothing's *wrong* with them. They're just, y'know, not the coolest thing to be named after."

"They're *totally* cool!" Joel cut in. Just like that, he'd lit up, like in the evening when all the streetlights come on at once. When Joel gets excited, he gestures with his whole body. "Butterflies are totally cool. Did you know some of them migrate over two thousand miles every year? We see a whole bunch of them in the woods around here. Aubrey knows all the names for the different kinds, but I forget. Aubrey, what was that black-and-white-striped one we saw the other day?"

I wished Joel would stop talking. I wished Joel would try to learn the middle school rules, the right and wrong topics to talk about at school. I kept thinking about the morning when Rudy Thomas had looked me up and down and Madilyn Sellers had giggled. *You're such a weirdo, Aubrey.*

"Zebra swallowtail," I kind of mumbled. Mari was never going to sit down at our lunch table again.

"Zebra swallowtail," Joel repeated, grinning. "You would've liked it. It was really punk. And we find tons of monarch butterflies, too, and then the ones that look like monarchs but aren't—what are those called again?"

"Viceroys," I mumbled even quieter. Joel didn't notice.

"That's it! They're not poisonous, but monarchs are, so the viceroy butterflies make themselves *look* like monarchs so nobody wants to eat them. Hey, Aubrey, remember the Mimic Elves?"

I did remember. After we'd learned about viceroys and monarchs from one of my field guide books, we'd added a special kind of elf in our Woodland

Elves game. It had been fun at the time. But now, as Joel told Mari all about the Mimic Elves at our lunch table at Riverview Middle, the game sounded silly. It sounded like something for little kids.

I went over my lists of right and wrong topics to talk about. Right topics: Which teachers are annoying. Which boys at school are cute. Which actors in which movies you want to see.

Wrong topics: Random facts about bugs. Random facts about plants. Pretend games in the woods.

I swirled my fork through the watery spaghetti on my tray while Joel kept going, telling Mari all about our Woodland Elves game. I waited for Mari to roll her eyes. I waited for her to get up and walk away.

But she finally said, "Okay, you've convinced me." Her mouth had twisted into a little bit of a smile. "Maybe butterflies aren't the worst thing to be named for."

Mari had gotten the handbook of the social rules, too—I saw her when she talked with the soccer girls or the other kids in our class. She *knew* which topics were right, and she could talk about them easy enough. But with Joel and me, she didn't seem to care when we got weird. She didn't care when we said the wrong things. I kept waiting for her to realize she could do better than us.

But she just stayed.

The more we got to know her, the more I liked Mari's name for a different reason. A butterfly is something that's already metamorphosed from a caterpillar in a cocoon and come out on the other side, fully formed. I figure that's the dream: to have already figured out what you want and who you are. To already be the person you're supposed to be.

Mari Clark-Espinoza moves through the world in a way that tells you that she *knows* herself, and she *likes* herself, and if you don't like her, you can just move right along thank-you-very-much. She already seems to have it all figured out.

I can't even imagine what that would feel like. I don't know what I want. I don't know who I am. I spent all year watching, trying to learn the middle school rules. Trying to be like Mari and the girls at school. Trying to act right.

But I don't think I've mastered it yet.

And here's another confession: Sometimes, I don't even think I want to.

I'm still half expecting for Mari to decide not to come with me on this trip after all. Sure, she's been friends with Joel and me for a whole school year, through the bullying and the visits to Vice Principal McDonnell's office, but she's always been friends with *us*—with Joel-and-me as a unit. But all year, it's been Joel and me, comma, and Mari.

I wait till we're almost to the edge of the woods before I finally make myself say it. "Are you sure you want to come?" I ask. "You don't have to."

"Yes, I want to," Mari says right away. She pushes the purple part of her hair back behind her ear. "And yeah, I have to, too. My moms..." She thinks for a minute, then shakes her head. "They've been saying all year that they want to help him. That he needs people on his side, at school and everything. And I know they *want* to help. But they've just been *talking*. It's not enough."

A breeze ruffles around us, and for a second it

cuts through the humidity and makes everything lighter. Easier to move through.

"So let's do it ourselves. Unless..." She pauses, and for a second something flickers across her face—a look of uncertainty I'm not used to seeing from her. She clenches her jaw, and the uncertainty goes away, but it makes me wonder if maybe Mari has a Cover-Up look just like Joel's, one that I haven't learned to see past very well yet. "Unless you want to do this by yourself," she finishes.

Joel's words from our fight the other night are playing back in my head. *My mom's been talking about getting out of Riverview for a while. I mean, she's* always *talking about it, but I think I'm gonna ask if we can finally*—The *we* he'd said then hadn't been Joel and me. It had been Joel without me. My stomach had started sinking, and sinking, and sinking....I kept waiting for the part where my stomach hit bottom, but it didn't come. It just kept sinking. It feels like it's still sinking now.

It's been just Joel and me for so long.

It's not that I want to go alone. It's just that, until

Mari said that she was coming, it hadn't occurred to me that I might not have to.

Say something, Aubrey.

"No," I say. "Please come."

Mari grins. When we're at my house again, we slip in through the back door and creep silently past Teagan's closed bedroom door, and we gather up food from the kitchen and the first aid kit from the bathroom. We dig my mom's good flashlight out of the kitchen junk drawer, just in case, and my red plastic compass from our old playroom. With all that piled in our arms, Mari and I sneak past Teagan's room one more time and head to my bedroom to grab my field guides and my backpack to stuff it all into—

Except that Teagan isn't in her room. She's in *mine*. She's pacing in front of my bed, her phone in her hand, staring up at me in the doorway like I just scared the living daylights out of her.

A CONVERSATION
I DON'T WANT TO HAVE

TEAGAN SCARES THE DAYLIGHTS OUT OF ME, TOO. I JUMP SO HARD I whack my elbow against the doorframe. It hits right on the funny bone, and tingles run up the length of my arm to my hand.

"Where've you been?" Teagan demands. Then she spots Mari in the doorway behind me and frowns. "Uh. Hi."

"Hi," Mari says.

"Where've you *been*?" Teagan asks again. She looks more than just scared—she looks *shaken*. She's still in her pajamas, shorts, and a T-shirt from her old volleyball team. Her finger is hovering over something on her phone screen. "I knocked on your door. To see how you…" She shakes her head. "And you weren't there. Where *were* you? I was about to call Mom and Dad."

"Don't call Mom and Dad," I say, too fast. Teagan's eyebrows go up. "I'm fine. We were just outside."

"Outside doing *what*?"

I don't answer her. I just rub my arm, trying to make the tingles go away.

"Okay," Teagan says. She lets out a breath, like she's trying to calm herself back down. She drops her phone hand to her side, but she doesn't put the phone away. "Okay. You're okay. And you've got Mari over. Hey, Mari."

"Hi," Mari says again.

"Mom said it was okay," I add. It's a little bit true but probably still counts as a lie of omission since I never actually asked Teagan's permission first. Oh well. I'll add it to the pile.

"Okay," she says again. I figure she's going to complain that she's got to watch both of us now or chew me out for leaving the house without telling her. But instead, her eyes go soft. She asks, "How're you doing?"

Teagan was born two years before me, and I notice the age difference sometimes more than others. When we were little, she'd pretend to be a pirate or a hero-in-training right alongside Joel and me. She used to run around the woods with us all the time, and she always found the best hiding spots when we played hide-and-seek. Once, she managed to hide herself *inside* a prickle bush. Not behind it. Inside. Even after we found her, I wasn't about to reach in there between the brambles and stickers and tag her out.

As we've gotten older, Teagan's stopped playing with Joel and me. She just finished eighth grade. She's going to start high school in the fall. She always wants to do less interesting things with her friends. Sometimes they sit around and talk in the big parking lot by the river at night. Sometimes they sit around and talk in our basement. Sometimes they walk over to Walmart and wander around for hours without buying anything.

I don't get what's fun about any of it, and I can't tell if Teagan actually thinks it's fun or if it's just what her friends want to do. Maybe when I'm about to start high school, I'll stop wanting to run around the woods, too. Maybe I'll suddenly enjoy sitting around, just talking about who likes who and who's dating who. Maybe I'll know all the right things to say. Maybe I'll stop feeling so weird and wrong and I'll be able to hide my secrets better.

Probably not, though.

The way Teagan asks "How're you doing?" is the same way everybody's been asking it since Joel left. It makes her seem really old all of a sudden. Two years feels like a long time.

"I'm fine," I tell her. I pretend that it's true. "Hey, we're gonna take a picnic lunch, I think," I say, nodding down at my armful of granola bars and bread loaf and peanut butter jar. "Is that okay?"

"It's ten in the morning," Teagan says.

"Well, we might go walking around for a while before we eat it."

"Ohhhh-kay." She draws out the word, makes the *oh* long and kind of judgmental. Like she's rolling her eyes at me out loud. Teagan never used to say "Ohhhh-kay" at me like that. "Mom says you aren't supposed to go in the woods," she says.

"I know."

"She says it might not be safe. Since we still don't know what happened to—"

"I *know*, okay?"

I don't mean to yell it. But it kind of comes out as a yell. I don't want Teagan to finish that sentence. I don't want her to say Joel's name out loud. For some reason, I don't want Teagan to point out that he's not here.

Nothing "happened to" Joel. Not exactly. That sounds like this wasn't something he chose. Like it wasn't something he actively did.

Like he didn't leave me behind.

"Are you sure you're okay?" Teagan asks.

"I'm fine!"

"Because I know it's a lot. Not just this, right now. I mean this whole year. I know there's been a lot going on, and I just... You've seemed..."

I don't want her to look at me. It feels like she's seeing too much.

Sometimes I like that my sister and I look similar, because Teagan looks confident and pretty and *right*. It feels like a possibility: Someday I guess I can look like that, too, if I decide to. Once I figure out all the rules about how to style my hair and how to wear makeup and how to paint my nails without wanting to peel off my own fingers every time I look at them afterward.

But sometimes I don't like that we look alike at all. Sometimes it feels like everyone's looking back and forth between the two of us and shaking their heads at my wasted potential.

"I don't know, A," Teagan says softly. *A* is her nickname for me. I kind of like it better than my full name, anyway. *Aubrey* has always felt like a name I'm pretending to be instead of a name I actually am. "I don't know."

I don't know, either.

I push past her into my room and drop my armful of supplies on my unmade bed. Mari does the same. My backpack's still sprawled in the middle of the floor, the place I dropped it when I got home from our camping trip. I unzip it, and Mari holds it open so

123

I can start shoving all our provisions into it, and all the while I can feel my sister watching us.

"Do you *want* to go back in the woods?" Teagan says suddenly. The way she says it makes me wonder if this is what she's been wanting to ask me all along. "I know Mom said not to, but I keep thinking about it. I mean, everybody was just out there yesterday, and it's got to be safe by now, right? And this would be... different. It might help to, you know, process everything. I miss him, you know?"

And I don't know why this is the first time it hits me that Teagan cares about Joel, too. Teagan spent years playing games with us in the woods. Joel is like a brother to her.

"You..." She shakes her head and tries again. "I don't know what it is exactly. But I can tell you're unhappy. And you've been unhappy for a while."

I dig my toe into a spot on the carpet, trying to focus on anything else so I don't have to look at her. The clock on my wall is ticking louder than usual. It feels like my heartbeat.

"And he helps," she adds. "Right?"

It's too much, she's too close to something, and I

want to be anywhere *but* here. But she says it gently. Not like the way she said *ohhhh-kay* earlier, not like she thinks I'm weird or she's rolling her eyes. She says it like my sister.

And I guess that's why I finally say, "Mari and me are going after him."

And why I add: "If you want to come with us."

Teagan stares. Her eyes bug out of her head like one of those rubber toys from the carnival with eyes that bulge when you squeeze its tummy. From behind me, Mari brushes her hand against the back of my elbow. She's reminding me she's there or giving me support, maybe.

"You know where he is?" Teagan blurts out.

"Not exactly. But..."

I don't even know how to say it. I think about that arrow made of sticks on the ground. Part of me wonders if I imagined it. If I was so desperate to find a sign of him by that creek, so desperate to find *anything*, that I made up a trail marker where there wasn't one.

But I decide to reach toward what I'm hoping for instead. "I think he wants us to follow him," I say.

I can feel Mari straighten a little beside me. Teagan opens her mouth to ask something, but I cut her off quick.

"You can't ask any questions, though," I say.

"What do you mean I can't—?"

"*No. Questions*," I say. "That's the rule. No questions if you want to come."

I'm not ready to explain it. I'm not ready to tell her everything, not when it feels like she's too close already. I truly don't know if I expect her to agree to the no questions rule or not. Mari is watching us, back and forth, like we're playing a game of tennis.

Finally, Teagan sighs again in that long *ohhhh-kay* way. But she shuts her mouth.

And she nods.

"Okay," she says. "Fine. Just give me a minute to get dressed."

OUT OF RIVERVIEW

WE DON'T TELL TEAGAN WHAT OUR PLAN IS. SURPRISINGLY, SHE DOESN'T push it. It's a relief, because the more I think about it, the more holes I see in the plan—holes I don't know how to fill. Even if we're checking in along the river every so often, we could pass Joel. We could end up looking for him farther along the Green than he's even made it. We could wander through the woods for days and be totally off track.

Would he have left me more trail markers? More arrows out of sticks, pointing us in the right direction? Even if he did, how on earth are we supposed to find them in the entire forest—along the whole length of the river?

The search party yesterday looked for Joel only in the woods inside Riverview. They didn't go any farther—they didn't know about the raft or the river. They don't know how far away Joel might go. Officer McCarthy has been talking to the sheriffs in all the counties around us, putting the word out to all the local businesses and neighbors and nearby communities to keep an eye out for him. Or at least that's what he told Joel's parents, who told my parents, who told me.

But Joel isn't going to just go walking into some grocery store two towns over. He's probably not even going to leave the woods. He's not going to risk going back to civilization if he doesn't want to be found, and he knows enough from my nature books and from our camping trips to be perfectly fine by himself in the woods.

Officer McCarthy doesn't know this, because Officer McCarthy doesn't know Joel.

As we pull on our muddy shoes and head out into the humid day, I tell myself this: It *feels* like we're going to find him. Taking the short route to catch up with him along the river feels right. The plan feels like it will work. It feels like I'm *supposed* to find him.

Doing something based on a *feeling* isn't usually like me. I like rules and plans. I like writing out steps and having justifications for each of them and backups for if the steps change.

Doing something based on a *feeling* is like Joel.

Mari, Teagan, and I don't go back into the woods. Instead, we set out through the front yard and along the street. We're taking the more direct route, and the more direct route is straight out of Riverview—it doesn't go through our patch of woods. Besides, we already know Joel isn't in *these* woods.

Since we're heading out along the regular old street, it feels like any other day. It feels like Teagan and Mari and me are walking to school or running errands. As soon as we get outside, my skin turns sticky. The sun starts to bake the back of my neck, and I can feel drops of sweat sliding down between my shoulder blades, under the back of my sports bra.

We walk through the streets of our neighborhood. The brick houses look mostly the same. They have just little differences between them: the Masons' house has bright blue shutters instead of white; the Petersons' is an extra half story taller than the others; the McEllisons' house has thick vines of ivy crawling up around the garage door. Joel's house is on the corner. Nothing really stands out about it. The grass on their lawn is neatly trimmed. His mom has hung a flower wreath on the front door. It looks pretty much like all the houses, except that I know it's Joel's.

The neighborhood is wide awake at this time of morning. Parents push strollers down the sidewalks. Little kids are riding their scooters around at the end of one of the cul-de-sacs. Mrs. Wendell, who goes to our church, is out in her front yard scattering mulch in her flower beds. She waves at us as we pass.

"Morning," she calls out. "Where're you girls headed today?"

Just like that, I see us like Mrs. Wendell must be seeing us: three girls out for a walk around the neighborhood. Teagan, with her high-waisted shorts and a pair of bright-rimmed sunglasses, looking like the cool high school girls who hang out at the pool all summer. Mari, with her punk purple hair and confident walk. And then me.

I feel like I'm pulling off a trick. Like just by being part of this group, I'm making Mrs. Wendell see me as a different version of me than... *me*.

I don't know if I like how well I can pull off the trick.

"Morning, Mrs. Wendell," Teagan says. "We're just walking. Just enjoying the day."

Mrs. Wendell focuses in on me and studies me a little too hard. "All right, sweetie?" she asks me. "All right?" is just another way of saying *How are you doing?* The mulch she hasn't spread over her flower beds yet is in a huge plastic bag in her driveway. It stinks like dirty towels.

"All right," I say.

THE FAMILY REUNION
LAST YEAR

HERE IS WHEN I REALIZED TEAGAN AND ME WERE DIFFERENT:

At the end of last summer, my parents made us drive up to Indiana for my mom's family reunion. She and my dad and Teagan and me drove five hours to go to a picnic shelter filled with a bunch of uncles and great-uncles and great-aunts and second-cousin-something-or-others. They're all related to me one way or another, I guess, but for most of them, I couldn't tell you how. All these supposed relatives piled the rickety picnic tables high with potluck foods: macaroni salad and potato salad and Jell-O salad and fruit salad and meatballs marinated in jelly sauce warming in a Crock-Pot.

My mom has brought us to the family reunion before. It's pretty much always the same. The uncle types make the same jokes over and over. The great-aunt types pat your cheek and ask you whether you're Patrick's or Hallie's kid. They ask you over and over about what grade you're in at school. For most of the reunion last year, I followed Teagan around. I let her answer the questions for both of us so I didn't have to talk as much.

Last year in particular, the great-aunt types fawned over Teagan. They all loved her *darling outfit* and her *darling hairstyle* and her face that *looks just like your mother's*. They all wanted to ask her about whether she had any boyfriends. *Beautiful. Just beautiful*, they called her.

After a while of admiring Teagan, one of the great-aunts—maybe a great-great-aunt—noticed me standing there, too. She looked me up and down and gave me a too-big smile.

"And this must be your brother?" she asked Teagan.

About me.

She thought I was Teagan's brother—she thought I was a *boy*.

My mom was close enough to hear. She swept in and clamped her hand on to my shoulder. "This is my younger daughter," my mom corrected the great-great-aunt with a smile. She put a little extra force on the word *daughter*. "Aubrey. She's going to be starting middle school soon."

"Oh," the great-great-aunt said.

"Middle school is always such an exciting time," another relative chimed in. But the first great-great-aunt was still blustering.

"The T-shirt. And the ponytail," the great-great-aunt said, nodding at my hair, which was pulled back in a low ponytail like always. "All the boys used to wear their hair that way back in my day."

"Lots of girls these days wear T-shirts and ponytails," my mom told her. Her fingers were rubbing my shoulder.

"Of course," the great-great-aunt said.

Another relative changed the topic, and I told myself to keep listening to the conversation, but

I'd gone far away. I was watching myself from the outside again. And yeah, my hair was pulled back in a ponytail that day, like always. And yeah, it was a different kind of ponytail than the kind Teagan sometimes wears her hair in. I had all my hair pulled back at the very bottom of my head because that's just where it falls; that's just where it feels normal. Whenever Teagan's tried to do my hair for me and put the ponytail up higher, it makes me feel weird until I pull it out.

And yeah, that day I was wearing a ratty T-shirt and jeans, and I was wearing the sports bra that pulled my chest in the most, and before that day I somehow hadn't thought that anybody noticed any of that. I hadn't thought that anybody besides me cared what I wore or how I did my hair or whether I looked enough like a girl.

Lots of girls these days wear T-shirts and ponytails. It's true. I knew it was true. But my stomach was fluttering like maybe I'd eaten too much Jell-O salad.

My mom had her hand on my shoulder. She probably figures I'll grow into everything—that I'm going to grow into being a nice, pretty girl like my sister. I don't know if I will. I don't even know if I want to. I knew her hand was supposed to be comforting, but instead it felt like she'd locked me in place. Like I couldn't escape. *I don't want to be here.* A funny, tingly feeling was running over my skin.

My brain just kept replaying the great-great-aunt saying, *This must be your brother,* and I couldn't figure out how it made me feel.

And maybe that was the worst part.

Because it didn't make me feel bad, exactly. It should have. I should've been able to say, *Actually, I'm her sister,* instead of waiting for my mom to swoop in. I should've *wanted* to correct her, to tell her I'm a girl.

But it hadn't made me feel bad.

It had just made me feel…*exposed.* Like I hadn't worked hard enough to cover myself up. Like someone had seen straight through me.

ANOTHER REASON JOEL LEFT

WALKING, IT TURNS OUT, GIVES YOU AN AWFUL LOT OF TIME TO THINK.

We head out of our neighborhood. Past the gas station on the main road. Past the house just beyond it that has the best Christmas lights every December. Past the traffic light, one of five in Riverview. Past the Church of the Sacred Heart, whose stained glass windows are glittering golden and turquoise and white in the morning sunshine.

Once we're on the outskirts of town, Mari's phone map points us along the highway. It's a little two-lane road so filled with potholes it looks like an asteroid landing site. There's no sidewalk, so we walk in the narrow edge of dirt between the asphalt and the grassy drainage ditch dug beside it. The water that runs through this ditch probably pools into Mystic Creek, too. It probably drains into the Green. Water leads to water leads to water.

We pass the sign marking the city limits of Riverview, but aside from that, it's a slow slide between town and countryside. The houses get farther apart. Huge cornfields and cow fields spread out over the hills. The corn all lined up in the fields has just barely started to sprout. In the cow fields, the cows just stand there, munching on the green grass, almost totally still except for their tails flicking every so often.

A few cars zip by us along the highway, but not many. The houses are so far apart now that sometimes, when we get between two hills, you can look in any direction and not see a single one. It's easy to pretend that we're the only people in the world.

And that's what I'm thinking about as we walk. About all the times Joel and I have felt like that. About how the woods feel like that.

About how we *needed* that this year.

Here is another huge reason I figure Joel ran away: Rudy Thomas.

Rudy Thomas has been in our class since kindergarten. He's always been a class clown, and he's always kind of annoyed me, but he hasn't always been a bully. At least I don't think he has. In first grade, he talked all the time when he wasn't supposed to and got our class in trouble on field trips. In second grade, he borrowed my pencil for art class once and then snapped it in half.

The snapping was probably an accident, even though I didn't think so in second grade.

The ways he teased Joel this year weren't accidents. But I didn't realize they were a big deal, until suddenly they were.

Sometimes, it would start in the hallway before school. Joel and I would be at our lockers, talking— sometimes with Mari or with other kids Joel knew from drama club, sometimes with just the two of us. Joel might be showing off the friendship bracelets he'd gotten from some of his little cousins, bright blue and lime green and neon yellow threads all knotted together. Rudy Thomas would be passing by with a couple of his friends. He'd say something like, "Nice jewelry, Gallagher. They really bring out your eyes."

Then he'd flutter his eyelashes, and his friends would crack up.

The first few times something like this happened, Joel would say, "Thanks for noticing, man, that's sweet." Joel's a really good actor—it's why he joined drama club and why he's so good at our games in the woods—and he'd say it with just enough earnestness that you couldn't really tell if he knew Rudy Thomas was making fun of him. Maybe he didn't know. Maybe Rudy Thomas *wasn't* making fun of him. To me, the whole thing always felt like a trap, but I couldn't pin down when or how the trap snapped.

Sometimes, the teasing would start in our fourth-period PE class. Joel is pretty bad at PE. Just about every class, he'd try to kick a soccer ball and swipe past it instead. Or he'd throw a football, and it would land barely ten feet in front of him. Or he'd get tagged out in the first fifteen seconds of a dodgeball game. Plenty of other boys in our class had a hard time with sports. Devin McBride was always tripping over the soccer ball or sometimes just his own feet, and I don't think Parker Ferguson caught a dodgeball all year.

But Rudy Thomas only cared when the person messing up was Joel. If Rudy was on Joel's team when Joel made a fumble like that, Rudy would groan and roll his eyes. If Joel was on the other team, Rudy would laugh. "God, Gallagher, you're such a girl."

Sometimes he wouldn't say "girl." Sometimes he'd say words that were worse.

Coach Nielsen, our PE teacher, might hear. He might say, "Second commandment, Thomas." We all memorized the Ten Commandments in Sunday school at the Church of the Sacred Heart. The second one is this: *Thou shalt not take the Lord's name in vain.* Nielsen would make Rudy Thomas run a lap around the gym for saying "God" like that. He never acknowledged the other words.

Sometimes, the teasing wouldn't start until lunchtime. Then, though, it was like Rudy had been saving up for it all morning. But he still wasn't a bully like you think of on TV. He didn't stomp around, beating kids up or taking their lunch money. Riverview

Middle has a zero-tolerance policy for bullying, or at least that's what Vice Principal McDonnell says, and except for giving him occasional talking-tos, McDonnell didn't do anything at all to Rudy Thomas.

If the teasing started at lunchtime, he'd pass by our table in the corner of the cafeteria and say something rude. He might sneer out a comment about how Joel only ever hangs out with girls. If he was really pushing it, he might say something about Joel being a "black sheep," since he's one of the few Black kids at Riverview Middle.

Then he'd slap Joel on the shoulder and laugh. Like it was all in good fun. Like he and Joel were buddies who were just joking around. For a split second, a look would skitter across Joel's face: a wilted expression I only made up a name for this year. Before this year, I didn't see that look enough to bother naming it.

This year, I started calling it the Hurt.

The Hurt never lasted long. Joel would smooth his face out into the Cover-Up Smile right after. As soon as Rudy Thomas left, Joel would go back to eating his mashed potatoes and telling Mari and me about something funny that happened in math class. But even in just the split second the Hurt look was there, it would've already been burned into my mind, like the flash from a camera making spots on the backs of your eyelids.

So Rudy Thomas isn't the only reason Joel left, but he was a big reason. He was the reason we started the Running-Away Game a couple of months into the school year. He was the reason Joel and me started sneaking out of school to build the raft. He was a big part of why sixth grade was so bad. He didn't go after me the way he went after Joel—in fact, after that morning with him and Madilyn Sellers right at the beginning of the year, he mostly didn't notice me at all. I was quiet enough that I flew under his radar.

If Joel and me really are the same kind of weird, the world sure treats us different. The things Rudy Thomas picked out about Joel, the ways he made Joel feel small, were some of the same things Joel's dad picked out, too. Just with different words. They both had these ideas about what kind of boy Joel was supposed to be. They both scratched at every place he didn't fit those ideas.

Joel was getting scratched at school by Rudy and at home by his own dad.

And maybe it was bigger than just those two people. Their ideas about how Joel was supposed to act didn't come from nowhere. I remember Rudy Thomas's dad snapping at Rudy in the parish hall. *Don't coddle him.* And *You don't see anyone else whining like a little girl.* That didn't come from nowhere, either. It's not just a couple of people who are the problem. It's everywhere.

Joel was getting scratched at all over the place.

HOW THE RUNNING-AWAY GAME STARTED

THE RUNNING-AWAY GAME STARTED IN NOVEMBER. BY THEN, I'D GOTTEN used to Mari sitting at our lunch table every day. I'd thought that having Mari around—having more than just me as backup—would mean Rudy Thomas would leave Joel well enough alone. But the day we started the Running-Away Game, all three of us were waiting in line for our trays of school chicken nuggets together—Mari and Joel and me—and it didn't change a thing.

I don't want to set down what Rudy Thomas said that day. It's something that doesn't bear repeating, as my mom would say. But when he said it, Joel's whole face crumpled. Then, a second later, his face went blank. It happened so fast I almost doubted I'd seen it—the Hurt look straight into a look as empty as a hole. Nothing there. No one home.

Rudy Thomas had said what he'd said like it was a joke, with a laugh in his voice and a smile in his eyes, and some of the kids around us in the lunch line laughed, too. It was hard not to. Even as I stared at Joel's blank face, even as anger started bubbling up in my stomach, I could feel the instinct to laugh bubbling in there, too. That's a confession. It was like the laugh was contagious. Rudy Thomas wasn't the slightest bit funny, but when you're nervous and startled and it's awkward and you don't know what else to do, and the people around you start laughing, it feels like the easiest thing.

I didn't laugh, but I hate that I had that instinct. I hate that I almost did.

After a couple of seconds, Joel grinned a little at Rudy Thomas, too, like he was in on the joke. Like it *was* just a joke. But it was his Cover-Up Smile. Even back in November, I could recognize that look a mile off.

Then Mari asked me a question about the chicken nuggets, her voice tight, and I scooted toward Joel a little so that Rudy Thomas was stuck behind me, and the lunch line started moving and Rudy Thomas wandered off. And that was the end of it.

Once we'd all gotten our food and claimed our usual table in the back corner, though, Mari slammed her tray into the tabletop. She slammed it so hard the table legs wobbled.

"What a *jerk*," she said. The way she said "*jerk*" sounded like she wanted to be saying something worse. "I *hate* him. Can I punch him? Joel, do you want me to punch him?"

"Not worth it," Joel said without looking up from his lunch tray. "Zero-tolerance bullying policy, remember?"

"*He's* the one being a bully," Mari fumed.

"We can at least report him to Vice Principal McDonnell," I said. She's got a stare that feels like knives.

"She won't do anything about it," Joel said.

"You don't know that," Mari said. "That really should be part of the zero-tolerance policy. He shouldn't get to say stuff like that. Maybe he'll get suspended."

"I *do* know that," he said. He was picking at his potatoes. He didn't say anything else about it. But Joel had already pulled me with him earlier that week when he'd reported Rudy Thomas for a different thing he'd said. He'd already reported him two other times this year. Every time, Vice Principal McDonnell had taken Rudy Thomas aside in the hallway to give him a thirty-second talking-to about showing respect for other people and not using "foul language." And that was it.

Now, though, in the lunchroom, Joel kept sticking his fork into his potatoes. He wasn't eating them. I nudged his shin under the table. When he didn't respond, I nudged him a couple more times till finally he looked up at me.

"You okay?" I asked, quiet.

Joel knew how good I am at reading his face. He didn't bother trying to hide his expression. He just looked at me. And I could see it all there: Hurt. Frustration. Anger. And tiredness. His dark eyes had bags spilling out underneath them. Even back in November, he looked worn out.

"I wish we could just get out of here," he said, going back to his potatoes.

I wasn't sure what he meant. I wasn't sure if he meant he wanted to get out of the cafeteria, or he wanted to get out of middle school, or he wanted to get out of Riverview. Out of this place we'd lived our whole lives and into something new.

I knew that tug. The *I don't want to be here* tug. Wanting to be someplace or someone else. It was what kept pulling me into our games in the woods.

That gave me an idea.

"Okay, so let's skip class," I said abruptly. "We don't need to go to pre-algebra. Where should we go?"

Joel picked up a lukewarm school chicken nugget and dropped it back on his tray. "Huh. Let's go to Wendy's."

"C'mon, think bigger."

"Okay, the Wendy's in Calumet."

Calumet is just the next town over. "Bigger!" I said. "I feel like you're not taking this seriously."

That made Joel smile a little bit. Mari had been watching us go back and forth, her eyebrows up. I don't usually talk a lot at school, and I definitely didn't talk much back in November. Now, she clapped her hands together, down to business.

"Canada!" she said. "We should go to Canada. I hear everybody's super polite there."

"I don't have a passport," Joel and I both said at the same time. We locked eyes. Joel's were glinting with the start of a laugh.

"No problem. We'll forge new papers for ourselves," Mari said. "I can be Duchess Sonia von Rasterburg, heiress of...something or other, and—"

"Ooh, can I be an heiress, too?" Joel cut in.

"Of course!"

"How are we going to get there?" I asked.

"Hitchhike?" Mari suggested. "Or stow away on a train?"

"We should get a boat!" Joel burst out. He was fully grinning now—a real one, one that made his eyes crinkle up. "Just a little one. We'll row across Lake Michigan! We can explore all the Great Lakes! We'll be like pirates!"

"I don't know if you can just sail in and out of the Great Lakes," Mari said. "I think there's waterfalls and dams and stuff in between them."

The only dam I knew was the old concrete one at Brownsville. My dad had let us stop and see it once on the way to Bowling Green when I was little. I remembered a gate system to let big boats get through, but I'd never thought about how smaller ones passed.

Joel had considered this for a minute. "When we have to, we'll just pull the boat out of the water and carry it over to the other side," he decided.

"Portage," I said.

They both blinked at me. For a second, the table was quiet, and I kicked myself. Wrong topic of conversation: using weird words you learned out of a nature guide book.

But I kept going. "That's what you call it when you take your boat out and carry it over land. Portage."

I waited for Mari to laugh or to say, *You're such a weirdo*, like Madilyn Sellers. But instead she was grinning, same as Joel. "Just how strong do you think we are? We're supposed to just carry our boat *and* all our stuff?"

"It's the power of teamwork!" Joel yelled out, so loud that the soccer players at the table next to us looked over, and for some reason that made us all three bust out laughing. We laughed so hard that soon half the cafeteria was staring at us. We laughed so hard that when we stopped, Joel's face barely had any residue from the Hurt look left on it.

We spent the rest of lunch like that, making wilder and wilder plans for our boat journey on the lakes and wilder and wilder plans for our new lives in Canada. And when lunch block ended, we went to class. We didn't actually skip. We didn't actually run away. That's what we did all year, whenever Rudy Thomas singled Joel out. We did it when someone made a comment about Mari's moms. We made up plans to run away to California and plans to run away to Iceland and plans to run away to South America. We made up plans to join the traveling circus and plans to start riding with a cross-country motorcycle gang. We came up with wild new identities for ourselves so we'd never be found: new names and new outfits and new lives.

And then, when we were done planning, we went to class.

Because it was just a game.

At least that was what I kept telling myself. It was all just a game. We were never going to actually *do* the plans we talked about.

Except that was never really true.

Joel liked the part of the game where we made all the plans to travel somewhere else: where we imagined visiting new places and seeing new sights and meeting new people. I just liked the part where we imagined getting *out*. Leaving everyone else who knew us and starting over someplace different. And I liked the part where we imagined turning ourselves into someone new.

THE WOODS

WE WALK ALONG THE HIGHWAY FOR AGES. OUR FOOTSTEPS CRUNCH IN THE grass. There's a rhythm to them if you listen long enough—all of us walking at the same speed but taking our steps at different times. The landscape keeps shifting back and forth between woods and fields. Sometimes we're surrounded by trees, and then the trees will thin out and there are houses again, or a barn nestled up on a hill. One house we pass has a row of little stone bunny statues lined up in the front yard. Another has a wheelless tractor out front, stacked up on cinder blocks. Another has a Confederate flag hanging over an upstairs window.

Mari makes a face and mutters a word at the house that, if I said it, would make my mom give me a scolding. But I agree with her.

Say something, Aubrey.

After a while, the houses shift back into woods again. The sun's high in the sky now, but our side of the highway is mostly in the shade. Blue jays call out to each other across the road.

"It's nice out here, isn't it?" Teagan says when we've been quiet for a while.

She says it a little surprised. Like she'd forgotten what it feels like to walk through the woods, even though we live right beside them.

"I get why you and him spend so much time out here," Teagan goes on. "Like, it's hot and sticky and there's bugs and snakes and spiders"—she gives a shudder—"but I get it."

"No, you don't," I say without thinking.

Her footsteps stop. When I glance over my shoulder, she's frowning. I kick at a rock, and it bounces into the road.

"What's that supposed to mean?" she says.

"Nothing. I don't know."

"No, really. I want to know. We're out here looking for Joel, and you won't even let me ask where he is, and—"

"I don't really want to talk," I cut in. "Let's just walk."

I'm mad at her, even though I don't really know why. I'm mad she's pretending like she can understand. When we were little, it felt like I could tell Teagan anything. It felt like she was one of the people who could see my weird and wouldn't care. Her and Joel both.

I don't know when that changed, exactly.

A couple of years ago, my family and Joel's family went camping together for a week. We rented a cabin at Mammoth Cave National Park. I'd been to Mammoth Cave tons of times before—it's pretty close to Riverview, and we go on a field trip there almost every year with school and take tours with the park rangers through different parts of the cave.

But that camping trip was the first time I'd really hiked in the aboveground parts of the park—in the woods. They're even greener than our woods in Riverview, somehow. The whole week while we stayed at the cabin, my dad would take Joel and Teagan and me out to explore the trails. Around the cabins, everything felt bustling and busy. There were tourists and RVs and little kids running around. But after just a couple of minutes of hiking, that all fell away. It was just us and the woods.

Mammoth Cave is the longest cave system in the world. Every year on our school tour, the park rangers tell us about how the land there is perfect for forming caves because it has two different layers of rock: limestone and sandstone. The sandstone is the stronger of the two, and it's on top. Limestone is softer, and it makes up the bedrock underneath. It's what makes sinkholes so common here. It only takes a little water before limestone starts to whittle away.

That's how the cave system formed. Over thousands of years, the Green River and all its little tributaries seeped into the lower limestone layer. They carved out bigger and bigger passages underground. The sandstone layer on top protected the cave passages and kept them stable. It kept them from collapsing.

I liked hiking the trails in the park. I liked knowing that there were miles and miles of cave system sprawling out underneath the ground. Partway through our camping week, we found a trail that went all the way up to the river, and my dad let us follow the water for a while, instead. We picked our way along the bank, over rocks and tree roots. The ground sloped up steep on either side of the river, cradling us.

We'd walked for ages before the river curved, and then the side across the water from us turned into a rocky cliff wall. The rocks were reddish brown and layered, sharp in some places, smooth in others. In one place, the rock dipped away into a dark cave opening. Even from across the river, I imagined I could feel cool air breathing out of it.

"Can we go in?" I'd asked my dad. "Please?"

My dad just shook his head. "I don't think so. We don't know where that goes, sweet pea. And none of us came prepared for spelunking."

But the little cave in the cliff couldn't have been connected to Mammoth Cave itself. Otherwise the park rangers would have boarded it off so nobody could wander inside and get lost and die. Probably this cave didn't go deep at all. The land there was perfect for making caves, after all—big or small.

I begged a while longer, and Joel joined in, too, until Teagan huffed out, "Why would you want to go in some creepy old cave, anyway? There's probably bugs."

"*Because* there's bugs!" I said. I'd been reading a lot about all the different kinds of cave beetles. The idea of finding one out in the wild made me so excited it felt like my chest might burst right out of my body.

Teagan had just wrinkled her nose at me. "You're so weird."

The words didn't hurt back then the way they did when Madilyn Sellers said almost the same ones. They just made me sad. Even back then, maybe I was starting to notice that Teagan and me were different. That there were things about me that Teagan and my parents just couldn't get.

My dad didn't give in, and so Joel and I gave up. Joel promised that we'd come back another time when we were older to explore the cave entrance. "Just the two of us," he'd said.

Now, as we hike along the highway, Teagan goes quiet for a while longer, but I can feel her fuming. I fume right back at her. The heat makes everything worse. Sweat keeps sliding down my forehead and into my eyes, and I can't wipe it away fast enough.

"I'm bored of just walking," Teagan says finally.

"We could play a game," Mari jumps in. "Instead of, you know. Talking. You and Joel play all kinds of games out here, right, Aubrey?"

The irritated fire inside me flickers again. "They're not like road trip games," I say. "Not, like, I Spy, or Cows and Graveyards, or anything. They're... different."

"I know. Joel's told me about some of your characters. You make up stories, right?"

Even now, I'm embarrassed that she knows about our games. I keep looking at my feet. I make my sneakers walk in a straight line just an inch off the edge of the road. Joel and I are too old for this. Everything's changing, and I'm supposed to be changing, and I'm supposed to be figuring out who I am and not wanting to run off to the woods to pretend to be somebody else all the time.

But I do want that, I guess. Secretly. I still feel most like myself when we're playing our games in the woods.

Sometimes I feel like the park at Mammoth Cave. Like there's a whole world of dark, winding cave passages underneath my surface. And like I'm going to spend my whole life just trying to build up that sandstone layer on top to protect it. To keep it all hidden. To stop my whole self from collapsing in like a sinkhole.

But Mari is still talking. "You have that Woodland Elves game, right? That sounded fun. You have the whole elf royal court and the elf army and everything. Who would I be in the elf world?"

Mari would probably be the general of the elvish army or a cool elf thief or something, but it feels too much to tell her that. "I don't know. Who would you want to be?"

"Maybe the royal adviser? Or a member of the guard?"

"I'd want to be some lesser member of the royal court," Teagan cuts in. "I don't want to have responsibility or have to make any big decisions, but

I still want people to bring me things and wait on my every need."

I watch her, waiting to see if she's making fun, but she meets my gaze, level. Teagan used to play games like this all the time with Joel and me. When we played Secret Agents, she used to be the team leader. When we played Pirates, she was the captain of the rival pirate ship we had to battle. When we played Percy Jackson, she was Annabeth.

Nowadays, she usually rolls her eyes at stuff like that.

This now, her joining in, feels like a peace offering. I nod at her. "You could be the grand duchess of the North," I say. "She's fourth in line for the throne. Maybe fifth." Joel would remember.

"Who would *you* be?" Teagan asks me. "Elf queen or something."

I make a face without meaning to. "No way."

"Elf king, then," Mari says without missing a beat.

She's looking at me with a little smile tucked in the corner of her mouth, and for a second I wonder if she's joking, but she's not. I know she's not. I feel like

I'm supposed to protest, to say *No way* to that, too, but...I don't know. I don't know.

"Yeah, sure," I say, still waiting for one of them to say no, to say I can't, because I'm supposed to be a girl, but they don't. We just keep going like that, talking about who else we'd have in our elvish court. When we've run through that, we talk about what decrees we'd make throughout the woods and how we'd handle diplomacy with the neighboring realms. It's not quite like playing the way Joel and me do. But it's close. It's still making up a story, like Mari said. It's still becoming someone else.

There's a warm feeling radiating through me now, and it's not from the humidity. It's a happy warmth. It feels like, ages ago, I swallowed ice water—like I drank it so fast it froze all down my throat. And now my insides are just starting to thaw back out. I'm just now remembering how they feel when they're not frozen.

It's Teagan playing along with us. It's Mari's little smile at me. It's realizing maybe not *everything* has to be a secret forever.

The woods thin out again after a while until they aren't woods anymore—they're just trees. Another row of farming fields, another row of houses. The sun overhead is scorching, and when I squint into it I can see an E-Z Mart gas station up ahead, and a few houses, and a little wooden church up on a hill.

We've made it to Calumet. We've hiked five miles to the next town over from Riverview.

We all go quiet when the sun hits our faces, when the town comes into view. Just like that, the game's over. Some things just work better in the woods.

CALUMET

"AIR-CONDITIONING," TEAGAN SAYS RIGHT AWAY, AND MAKES A BEELINE for the E-Z Mart. I hesitate. Strolling into a store just one town over from ours seems like a really good way to get recognized by someone who would ask questions about what we're doing out here—and probably call our parents. But the E-Z Mart looks quiet enough. The gas pumps out front stand empty. A handful of dusty cars and pickups are parked beside the building.

Mari and I glance at each other, and another drop of sweat slides down into my eye, and I have to admit that standing in the chill of an air conditioner for a couple of minutes sounds nice.

The bell over the glass door chimes as we push inside, and the older guy at the cash register nods at us. The cold air hits with a whoosh like opening an air lock. Mari meanders off down one of the aisles, and I trail behind her, not really looking for anything in particular. Teagan heads to the refrigerated section at the back, even though we've already got food and water with us and we didn't bring any money—or at least I didn't. She's just opening each fridge door for a second, letting the burst of cold air hit her in the face, and then closing it again.

I glance up toward the front counter to see whether the cashier is glaring at her. I figure he's probably not happy about a bunch of kids coming into his store and wasting the refrigeration. But he's busy with a customer.

Then I look closer, and I freeze.

It's Joel's mom at the counter.

She's talking to the guy at the cash register—she must've been off in the shelves when we came in. Now she's showing the cashier a square of paper in her hand. A note? A photo? *Joel's* photo? My stomach clenches up. When she was talking to me outside the

166

church, she mentioned that she was "asking around" about Joel—is this what she meant? Does she know Joel came through this way? Is she out here to track him down, just like we are?

That thought makes my stomach clench even tighter. I'm remembering what Joel told me by the campfire that night, and the way his mom said my name yesterday, serious and gentle and hard to look away from, and all I can think is *He's leaving me, he left me*, and I don't want to be here....

I duck back behind a wire rack of beef jerky sticks and Hostess cupcakes before Joel's mom can see me. I don't know where Mari and Teagan are. Don't have time to find them. Joel's mom will most likely recognize Mari, but she'll *definitely* recognize me and Teagan, and then it's phone calls to our parents and having to explain ourselves, and it's so much more than that, anyway. I don't want to deal with it. I don't want to deal with *her*. I hurry for the E-Z Mart door, push it open—

And remember too late that it's got one of those jingly bells over it that rings every time it opens.

The cash register guy and Joel's mom both look

up toward the noise. For just a second, my eyes lock with Joel's mom's. Eyes like Joel's, expression like Joel's. Her mouth opens to say, "Aubrey—?"

But I'm already sprinting out the door and around the side of the building.

I'm done. Caught. She's going to come after me. My heart's racing as I frantically search for someplace to hide. There's nowhere to go out here—just the empty gas pumps and empty cars and empty expanse of parking lot. A little farther down the road, a wooden church stands up on the hill, looking more like a log cabin than a church except for the big wooden cross hanging over the front porch. No stained glass windows or fancy steeple like the Church of the Sacred Heart. Just four walls and a sign planted in the front lawn that reads *Saint Sebastian Catholic Church*.

I race up the hill toward it, digging my shoes into the grass. Pushing off hard with every step. I worry that the doors will be locked, but it's a church and it's Kentucky, as my mom would say—it's got good small-town hospitality. The big wooden door swings open for me, no problem, and swings shut again behind me.

And just like that, the world goes quiet and my heart stills. Falls back into a slow, steady beat. The dusty carpet under my feet muffles all sound. I've spent a good chunk of my life so far in church—every Sunday, of course, and on all the holy days of obligation, and sometimes for extra services during Lent, and sometimes with my grandma Sadie when she brings me and Teagan there on special days for the sacrament of confession. But I'm almost never inside a church when there isn't a service happening. I'm almost never inside a church when there isn't quiet organ music piping overhead and the *shuffle-shuffle* of kids flipping through the hymnals in the next pew. I'm almost never inside a church when it's just *me*.

Without really thinking about it, I kneel down on one knee, make the sign of the cross with my hand, just like you do before Mass. I slide onto the seat. Hands folded in my lap. There's no bored Jesus to stare at on the crucifix over the altar like back at the Church of the Sacred Heart. The wood mounted on the wall at the front of the church isn't a crucifix at all—it's just a plain old cross.

I should try to hide myself better. I should duck under a pew or find a side room or something to wait in. Joel's mom might've spotted me running up here. If she did, she'll definitely come looking for me.

Instead, I just sit there in the pew.

I've never been very good at praying. Most of the time I feel like I'm faking it—like I'm praying because I know I'm supposed to but not because I really feel like God's listening. Most of the time, praying feels a little like playing pretend.

I like praying the rosary, though. My grandma Sadie gave me a rosary for my First Communion back in second grade, and sometimes I use it when I'm lying in bed, trying to fall asleep. I count my way through each of the sets of ten beads, and I count my way through the set of prayers in between, and I think about the holy mysteries of the rosary we learned about in Sunday school classes at Sacred Heart.

"Of *course* you like the rosary," Joel said a couple of years ago when I told him that. "It's like a praying checklist. You say your Our Father and you check that one off, and you say all your Hail Marys and check all those off, and you say your Glory Be, and then you get to start checking them off all over again. It's basically a huge to-do list of prayers."

He was rolling his eyes when he said all that, but he was grinning a little, too. Joel knows how much I like lists. And maybe he's right. I like saying the same words over and over in my mind. I like the feeling of each rosary bead in between my fingers, helping me keep count, and I like sliding from one bead to the next with each prayer until I make it all the way around the string. I like the way it all falls into a rhythm—I'm just being. I'm just existing.

So instead of hiding, or even instead of praying, that's what I do now: I just breathe. I just exist.

The church is so quiet it presses on my ears. It seeps into my brain. When I try, I can still hear the thrum of an air conditioner and the occasional rumble of a car on the highway far away. But I can also let it all fade out. It feels like I'm just me, like there's nobody else around to worry about me or to judge me or to see me in a way that's different from how I see myself.

It feels like the woods.

THE RAFT

WHEN WE SNUCK OUT OF SCHOOL THAT FIRST TIME, THE AFTERNOON NEAR the end of the year when we built the fairy rafts, I didn't know what we were starting. Joel had first suggested it during our sixth-period English class, when Mrs. Escobar was going to make us read *A Midsummer Night's Dream* out loud the next day— she said we needed an introduction to Shakespeare before we started seventh grade. She was assigning us parts.

Two seats in front of Joel, three seats in front of me, Rudy Thomas was skimming through the list of characters. He dragged one finger down the page in our English book. "*Titania*," he read, sounding out the syllables. "*Queen of the fairies*. Heh. That'd be a good one for you, Gallagher."

Joel pretended not to hear. He just kept doodling in his notebook.

"Gallagher," Rudy Thomas said, louder. He reached way back and poked Joel in the top of the head with his pencil till Joel looked up. "I said you should play the queen of the fairies. Since you're so good at, you know. *Acting.*"

Joel's face peeled into a grin, and he laughed it off. He looked tired. "Ha. Yeah. Good one, man."

Mari didn't have that class with us. She wasn't there to step in. So I asked Joel, "Hey, did you write down the homework assignment?" so Joel would have an excuse to turn away until Rudy Thomas got bored and left him alone. It was all a routine by that point. We knew our jobs.

But even as Joel listed off the homework for me to write down, I couldn't shake the feeling that Rudy Thomas was making fun of me, too. Even if he didn't know it. Even though he hadn't really said a word directly to me since the start of the year. My ears

173

were buzzing a little bit, and I had that faraway feeling, watching myself from outside myself. I wanted to be anywhere but in English class. I didn't want anyone to know that before Rudy Thomas had said what he'd said, I'd been looking down the character list, too, thinking that maybe I'd surprise everyone and ask Mrs. Escobar if I could read for Puck. Even though I couldn't tell if Puck was a girl's part.

After Rudy Thomas said what he said, though, I kept my hand down. If Joel was wrong for being who he was, for liking what he liked, then I was wrong, too. I was just quieter about it.

Just better at keeping the secret.

I thought that was that, and we all moved on. But a few minutes later, Joel turned around again in his desk to face me. "Let's get out of here."

"Okay," I said. I thought he was playing the usual Running-Away Game. "Where to this time? Canada or Mexico?"

"No, let's *really* get out of here," Joel said. "I mean it. Nobody'll notice. Or if they notice they won't care. They'll figure we're in the office or something. It's just two classes left. I just...I don't want to be here."

I looked at him fast. For a split second I wasn't sure if he'd really said it or if I'd just thought it. It was like he'd pulled the thought from my brain. Something was different in his tone, or maybe on his face. I couldn't quite place it. His face was a mix of the Hurt look and the Cover-Up look with an added mix of seriousness that I didn't see very often.

"Okay," I said again, but slower.

"How do we get out of school without getting caught?"

We'd never played this part of the Running-Away Game before. But I'd thought about it.

I thought about it all the time.

Here's the thing about having a secret, or *being* a secret: It's exhausting. And it's scary. And you always have to be ready to run, to escape, in case it becomes too much. Even if you don't know where you're escaping *to*. You're always looking around, looking for all the ways out, just in case.

I'd spent enough time wanting to hide away and not have to deal with sixth grade and not have to handle people seeing me, to have formed an escape route from every room of Riverview Middle School.

"Over the fence by the science annex," I said. The science annex at Riverview Middle is in a different building than the rest of the classrooms. The buildings aren't even connected. You have to go outside to travel between them. A crumbly sidewalk leads from the main building out to the annex. Chain-link fences close it in on either side, but they're practically asking someone to climb up them. Those fences have always felt to me like a dare.

"Okay," Joel said, thinking it out. Then, "Okay. Yeah. Okay, then what?"

We talked it out. Every piece of the escape plan I'd been forming all year without even really meaning to. The science annex fence, and then around the corner of the building. We'd wait there till the bell rang, crouched low so we weren't visible from the classroom windows, and then in the chaos of changing classes we'd take off across the football fields behind the school and into the woods.

The plan worked just like I'd always imagined it, and we spent the afternoon building our fairy rafts and goofing off. I thought it was a onetime thing, that our first time of sneaking out of school would be the *only* time. We only had two more weeks, after all, and then a whole summer of playing in the woods.

But the coming summer had started to look different. I didn't know if this summer would be like the summers every year before. Joel's parents had been fighting a lot. Teagan had started to look at me different. I didn't know if Joel and me would get to still spend our whole summer playing, or if we were too old.

Our games were starting to lose that feeling—like they mattered, even though they were pretend. Everything felt different.

The morning after the fairy rafts, we met at our lockers before class like we always do. Joel's eyes were bright and full of energy—I recognized that one as his I've Got an Idea look.

"Did you get in trouble?" I asked him. "For sneaking out yesterday?"

"Nope. My parents didn't even know we left. You?"

"Nope."

"Hey, I was thinking," Joel said. "What if—"

But before he could say whatever he'd been

thinking, Mari spotted us from down the hall and beelined our way. She dropped her backpack against the rusty gray lockers at my feet. "Hey, where were y'all yesterday? I didn't see you after school. Did your homeroom let you out early or something?"

Mari didn't have very many classes with either of us this year. Just social studies with me, and that was in the morning. She hadn't been in either of the classes we'd skipped the day before, and somehow, as Joel and me were scaling the fence and running across the football field and making fairy rafts, I didn't even think about Mari wondering where we'd gone. I didn't think we'd be missed.

"We were—" I started.

But Joel cut in. "In the office," he said. "Had to meet with the guidance counselor."

Joel and I both spent some time in the guidance counselor's office this year—him more than me. The guidance counselor is a middle-aged woman named Mrs. Harrison, with shoes that click on the linoleum and skin paler than the inside of a potato. She's nice enough, but she gives too much advice that doesn't

178

mean anything, like, *Let's look at it from another perspective*, and *That sounds like a good challenge.* All year, she liked to call Joel to her office because of the bullying, even though she never *said* he was getting bullied. She called it "not fitting in." She liked to call me in because she wanted to help me "come out of my shell." Or at least that's what she told my mom and dad in the notes she wrote home.

So Joel and me getting called to Mrs. Harrison's office at the end of the school day was a believable enough story. But Joel was making his I'm Lying face—eyes focused on a point somewhere off in the distance, hands picking at each other. He knows I can read it, so he doesn't bother trying to lie to me. I don't lie to him, either, at least not outright. And I don't think he can recognize my Lying By Omission face.

Mari couldn't see his I'm Lying face, though. Or if she did, she didn't point it out.

"Oh," she said. "Everything okay?"

"Yeah," Joel said. "It's dandy."

Mari didn't seem to catch that one, either, but it

was another tell. Joel only says things like *It's dandy* when he's lying. When he's lying, he starts talking like my grandma.

Joel and me didn't talk any more that morning about our sneaking out of school. We didn't talk about it at all during classes. Not in the hallway, either. Not during lunch.

We might not have talked about sneaking out of school any more at all, except that, after lunch, when Mari had headed to her class and Joel and me were getting our books out of our lockers, Rudy Thomas and James Todd passed us. And Rudy and James muttered something to each other, just loud enough for us to hear but just quiet enough to pretend that we weren't *supposed* to hear.

And then Rudy jumped at Joel with his hands up, like he was about to grab him. Or hit him. Or worse. He stopped well short of him. But Joel flinched all the same.

Rudy and James busted out laughing, and Rudy punched him on the arm in a way that would've been friendly from somebody else. Not hard. Joel flinched again.

"God, Gallagher. You're jumpy," Rudy Thomas said.

Say something, Aubrey. But I didn't. Neither of us said a word. Rudy Thomas and James Todd left. Joel went back to rummaging through his books, but his shoulders under his T-shirt had hunched up.

We both walked to English class without talking. As soon as we sat down, though, Joel turned around in his desk to face mine. "I was thinking," he said. "We could build a real one. You know?"

"A real what?" I said.

"A real raft. Not just a fairy one. Like, we could build a real, person-sized raft. People do that, you know? I found this article online. You just build a frame, and then a platform for it, and something to keep it afloat—"

"You're joking," I said. I really thought he was.

"No, really. I was thinking we could use inner tubes for the floating, maybe? Like the kind you use for tubing on the river? I think my uncle's got one."

"You're serious? About building a raft. An *actual* raft. You're serious?"

"As a heart attack," he said.

Joel's always taken ideas and run with them. When he gets an idea in his head, he can't let it go. It's like the ghost-hunting or the cupcake-making all over again.

I tried to tell myself the raft was just another of his wild ideas. But maybe I got it, too. Building a raft felt the same as our Running-Away Game: exhilarating, exciting, tugging at me like a string.

"Yeah, okay," I said finally. "We can try it, I guess."

Joel kept telling me about the article he'd read, and about the supplies we'd need to build it, and about where we could find them. He said the raft could be our summer project—that we'd start building it after school let out and by August we'd be done.

We weren't going to do anything else about it that day.

But just a few minutes later, during that same class, Rudy Thomas said *the word* at Joel—*the word* that I don't want to repeat. It made Joel's face go hollow.

We didn't wait till summer. After the bell rang, Joel and me climbed the fence by the science annex just like we had the day before. We ducked under the windows. We sprinted across the football field. We hid in the woods.

Every day for those last two weeks of school, that became our routine: run away to the woods and build our raft.

SOME ACCIDENTAL ARSON

LITTLE LIGHTS ARE DANCING AROUND THE WOODEN CHURCH IN CALUMET. They're flickering off the back of the pew in front of me, reflected in its smooth finish. I turn around. Along the back wall of the church, a small side table has rows and rows of prayer candles lined up on a stand. Some of the candles are burning. But a lot haven't been lit. They make me think of the candles we used at the vigil for Joel: skinny and white, planted in little cups. There's a box of matches on the table and a fancy-looking purple cloth draped over a little bench, a place to kneel and pray.

I pad across the carpet and wipe my hands,

dusted with dirt from hiking through the woods, on my shorts. The Church of the Sacred Heart has prayer candles like this, too, but I've never lit one. I guess I've never had a reason to. Tiny spirals of smoke curl upward from each candle and disappear into the air.

I strike a match.

It takes me a couple of tries. Strike it against the side of the box, watch the spark, but then nothing. It sputters out. I try again—strike, spark, nothing. On the third try, I do it harder, a solid *fwick*—and then there's a flame there, warming my fingers. I light a candle right at the front of the table, and then I stand there, watching the light flicker for a second and then steady out.

I have to find him, I think.

I don't know if I'm praying or thinking. Sometimes I don't know if there's much of a difference. When I'm praying the rosary or saying a prayer I've memorized the words for, that's one thing. But praying from the heart is something different. It's just talking to God, the same way you'd talk to yourself, I figure.

Please help me find him, I think. *I need him. And I let him down.*

That part feels impossible to admit out loud yet, but it's easier just thinking it. I'm remembering Joel's words by the campfire that night: *Say something, Aubrey.*

I let him down, I think. *I wasn't there when he needed me. And I don't know how to fix it, except that the first step is to find him.*

And another thought flickers through my mind:

I don't know how to fix me.

I've spent so long in church wondering what's wrong with me. I figured everyone does, right? Every Sunday at Mass, you ask God for mercy for your sins. Every time you go to confession, you have to pray first and think about everything you've done wrong that you need to ask forgiveness for.

But for a while now, I've had a hunch that there's something wrong with me that's not something I've *done*. It's something I am. And I don't know how to ask forgiveness for that.

And I don't know if I *want* forgiveness. Or need it.

Or if all I want is to understand.

Right then, the door to the church slams open right beside me. Mari's head pops around the corner.

"Aubrey? You in here?"

I jump. Like I'm getting caught doing something I shouldn't. Like she might see my secret, that there's something wrong with me, written there in the candle smoke.

And my butt whacks against the edge of the prayer table.

And the candles wobble.

And three of the candles on the farthest edge—not one, not two, but *three*—all wobble and wobble and don't catch their balance, and I know what's going to happen a second before it does, and I expect time to slow down, but instead it speeds up, or it skips a second, and I barely even see them falling: just one minute they're on the table, and the next minute they're on the floor instead.

The three candle flames hit the carpet, and it starts to smoke right away.

"Oh, *shoot,*" Mari says. But she doesn't say *shoot.* She says the swear word. Right there in the doorway of a church.

She races inside with Teagan right behind her, and I'm just standing there staring—can't move, can't even breathe—and out of all the bad things I've done in the last couple of weeks, running away from school and lying to my parents and lying to the police and letting Joel down—even out of all that, this is probably worse.

Maybe there really *is* something wrong with me. Because here I am, about to burn down a church.

The charred spot on the rug is turning into an actual fire, orange and creeping at the edges, and Teagan is yelling, "What do we do, what do we *do*?" and Mari is swearing and I'm remembering the firefighter who came to our class every year of elementary school for Fire Safety Month—how he'd always tell us to *stop, drop, and roll*. But that's only for when *you're* on fire. He never told us what to do when a house of God is.

"Smother it," I burst out. "We have to smother it!"

Mari and me both snatch at the purple cloth draped on the kneeler and throw it over the fire. We stomp on it. Stomp on it some more. Stomp on it till the soft, velvety fabric is covered in our muddy shoe prints, till it's crumpled and dirty and mashed and a little charred—

But then it's okay.

It's charred, but it's not burning.

The fire is out.

Mari and Teagan are both staring at me. Mari's face is alight. Her eyes are dancing, and her purple-streaked hair is all over the place, and she looks like she's about to bust out laughing. And that somehow makes me want to start laughing, too. I'm probably going to go to hell for starting a fire in a church, but it's out now, and for some reason it's all hilarious.

It only lasts a second before a voice says, "What is *happening* here?" and my brain says, *Run.*

A woman is standing at the front end of the room, a hand over her mouth. And it doesn't take much detective work to tell she's a woman of the church. She looks like my grandma Sadie. She's an elderly white woman with permed white hair, an ankle-length skirt, and a look of horror on her face as she takes in the three of us, the prayer candles on the floor, and the stomped-on purple shroud.

"C'mon," I'm already saying, grabbing for Teagan's and Mari's arms to pull them toward the back door. I'm making an escape plan without even thinking

189

about it: out the door, across the lawn, into the next patch of woods just beyond Calumet.

But when we push through the door, we run directly into Joel's mom.

She blinks down at me, her eyes wide. "*There* you are," she says. "Aubrey, what's—?"

I can't stop. I take off again. Push past Joel's mom. From somewhere behind me, Teagan says, "A, wait—" but I latch on to her wrist and drag her with me. Across the lawn. My feet pound into the dirt, Mari's and Teagan's footsteps right behind me. Past the last few houses of Calumet. Toward the tree line. We don't bother to look for a trail—we just crash straight through the trees, straight through the underbrush. We run with ivy tickling at our ankles and spiderwebs catching in our hair.

We run until we're deep enough that we're hopefully out of sight, run until my lungs feel about to fall out. And then we collapse on the forest floor, panting and gasping and clutching at our ribs. I can't decide whether I want to laugh or throw up. I just lie there on my back, looking up at tree branches over our heads.

And I breathe.

In the tree above us I spot wide green leaves, five lobes on each. It's a maple. I've got a couple different varieties in my leaf collection at home. I scan the other trees around us and let my brain list off the names I know so well. Hickory. Red oak. I even find the hairy-looking acorns of a bur oak, just like the one leaning over Mystic Creek.

The names help my brain go quiet. This is my favorite thing about the woods. The woods are mysterious and magical, but they're also orderly. They've got an organization to everything if you know how to find it. I like how all the trees, all the plants, all the birds and butterflies and ants crawling along the branches have names. They all have labels. Classifications. If you don't know the name, you can find it in a field guide. You can learn everything about it. You can find *answers.*

People are more complicated. With people, I never know exactly where I stand. Every person, every conversation, I feel like I'm missing a step.

People don't have simple answers.

Teagan breaks the silence between the three of us first. "We have to go back," she says.

I sit up fast. Too fast. For a second, the maple trees and bur oak and forest around me go fuzzy. "What?" I say.

"This is wild. Why can't we tell his mom we're out looking for him?"

"You're not allowed to ask questions," I say. My chest's gone tight. "That was the rule for you to come with us. Remember?"

Teagan makes a groaning sound like an angry bull. "Come *on*, A. I have questions. I'm pretty sure I get to ask them at this point."

A hot feeling's expanding out from my chest, too big for my body, and I want to scream. The worst part is that Teagan's right. She's walked miles with us already on pure faith, and she deserves to know the story. Joel's mom does, too. So many people around us have been saying one thing and meaning another, but Joel's mom never has. I just didn't want to hear the things she was saying.

I know it in my gut that I'm not being fair to either of them.

But there are parts I'm not ready to tell, and parts I know they're not going to understand, and parts I don't have the right answers for yet. And mixed in with all of it is a lurking suspicion that this is what happens when you're a secret: you let people down. I hate it. I *hate* it.

I just keep seeing the nameless look on Joel's face after our fight by the campfire.

"You know how to find him," Teagan says. She's looking at me too close again, and it's not a question. Not anymore. "A, we have to go back and tell his mom. What were you thinking? She's been freaking out. I only came with you because I knew you were gonna go anyway, but we've been out here for hours. We need help. From her, and from Mom and Dad. We can't do this all on our own!"

Joel and me have been doing pretty much everything on our own these days. We went camping on our own. We built the raft on our own.

Look how that all turned out, a small voice in my mind says, but I ignore it.

"We're going back," Teagan says again. Decided.

I can't read her face one bit. Teagan isn't like Joel: I can't decode her every eyebrow raise and every head tilt and every twitch of her mouth. I can't look up what she's feeling in a field guide. My sister is growing and changing into a person I don't quite understand. A person I maybe want to be like, or am *supposed* to want to be like, but also don't want to be like at all.

But I guess I don't know everything about Joel, either. No matter how much we've grown up together. No matter how many names I've made up for his different faces.

"Okay," I say finally. "Okay. Fine. You're right. We can go back."

But it's a lie.

Calumet isn't far—separated from us just by a thin ribbon of woods. The trees stretch out around us in all directions. Teagan studies me, and for a second I think she's going to know. I think she can tell I'm a liar. But she looks from me to Mari and back to me, and finally she nods.

"Good," she says. "We can probably still find his mom in Calumet. We'll tell her everything we know. She can decide what to do from there."

And she turns to head back.

Behind her, Mari and I lock eyes, and I have a sudden sinking feeling that Mari wants out of this, too. That she's on Teagan's side and wants to go back for help instead of forging ahead.

But instead, Mari nods at me, small, and then she nods at the empty expanse of woods behind us. Away from Teagan and Joel's mom and Calumet. Toward the river and the raft and *Joel*. She already knows I was lying.

And she's coming with me.

I nod back.

To the river? she mouths.

We've been hiking through the right woods, heading in the right direction, but we haven't gone to the water yet. It's time. I don't know what I'm expecting to find there. But it's time to head a little farther north and stop in along the Green.

I nod again.

Mari and I take off running.

By the time Teagan notices we aren't there—by the time her voice yells after us, "Hey! *Hey!* What are you doing?"—we're already crashing through the woods again. Diving deeper into the trees. Heading somewhere new.

Away, away, away.

OFF-TRAIL

MARI AND ME DON'T SLOW TO A STOP TILL IT'S JUST WOODS ALL AROUND us. No sign of people at all. We're officially off-trail.

I never go in the woods without following a trail. You're not really supposed to—it's terrible for the environment to have people hiking through the underbrush, trampling vines and moss and animal dens all over the place. I didn't have time to worry about it when we were running from the church and then running from Teagan. Now, though, I say a silent apology to the woods for disturbing everything that lives here.

Mari pulls out her phone again. It doesn't have

cell signal, but it still shows our blue dot moving on the map she downloaded. The river's to the north of us, a blue ribbony line.

Back when we studied the Green River in school, Joel liked to trace out shapes in the river's loops on the map. He'd find shapes in it the way people look for shapes in clouds. There's one spot where the river's line hooks over and makes an outline of a bird with a long, pointy beak. Another spot where it looks like a bunny rabbit: A wide curve forms the bunny's tail and its back, and then a long stretch of river cuts up north for the ear, bending back down after to make the bunny's rounded face. There's even an island in the river right where the bunny's eye would go.

We're a little under the loop of the bunny rabbit's head. As Mari and me start walking, we adjust so our dot on the map moves toward the line of the river. I angle us more north than we need to go, so that when we reach the water, it'll be right by the bunny's eye. It's silly, I know. But it feels like a little tribute to Joel.

We're still too close to Calumet for comfort for us to stop to eat lunch, but Mari and I munch on bread and granola bars as we walk. I'm too jittery to eat much, anyway. The sun's shifting in and out of the branches overhead. The air feels damp here, but less sticky, somehow. It has the cool, earthy smell of the world after rain.

I hear the river first, hardly louder than the breeze. Ahead of us, the ground slopes, and then we can see where the land meets the water.

We learned in school that the Green River isn't named for the color. It's named for a person: Nathanael Greene, a general back in the Revolutionary War. Even so, the name matches. I read somewhere that the river gets its color from the plant life underneath the water's surface. The Green is full of interesting fish and mussels and algae. But I like to think another reason the river's so green is because it reflects back everything that's around it: trees and trees and trees.

"Okay," Mari says. Down to business. "What are we looking for?"

Honestly, I don't know. Maybe I have a wild hope that Joel would've looked at the bunny's eye on the map, too, and would've decided to stop here. Maybe I'm hoping he left me another trail marker—if the stick arrow back in Riverview even *was* a trail marker. Maybe the sticks were just sticks. All I can do is feel around for our tin-can-telephone string, praying that maybe it's not so severed after all.

It's all such a long shot.

"A campsite, I guess?" I say, even though I know Joel would clean up his campsite behind him. "Or litter." He'd clean up his litter, too. "I don't know. Let's just walk along it for a while."

We set off along the bank. Mari moves slow, nudging the toes of her shoes in the grass as she goes, like she thinks she might kick into some magical sign that Joel Gallagher was here. I keep looking over at the water, staying a few steps ahead of her.

"You told Teagan earlier that you thought he wanted us to follow him," Mari says. "Was that true?"

She can tell I've been lying one way or another. Either lying to Teagan for saying it, or lying by omission to Mari for not telling her about the trail marker. But I don't even know what the truth is. I don't know an answer for sure. Even just admitting that in my own head makes my chest clench up, turns my palms sweaty.

"Maybe," I say. "I don't know. Just a gut feeling."

"Okay," she says, but she leaves the word open somehow. Like she knows there's more I'm supposed to say.

I keep trying to figure out a better way to answer, but I finally give up and we just keep walking. Birds are singing through the trees: A robin sends out a high, squeaky trill. Another bird answers with a long note, and then a fast *pew-pew-pew* sound—I see a flash of red through the branches overhead. A cardinal. Joel and me used to lie on our backs in the grass for ages, listening to the birds in our woods. Learning what each of their calls sounded like.

Up ahead, there's a mound of something piled on the ground. Stones. Something tugs me toward it. I pick up my pace, not sure if Mari's following me, not sure if I can trust the bubble of excitement that's starting to grow in my chest, just like when I found the stick arrow.

But there's no imagining this one. It's another trail marker.

The stones beside the river have been carefully

stacked into a tower. It comes up almost to my knee. Joel and I would always leave this one, this mound of stones, as a signal to the other that you were on track. You were going the right way. *Keep going.*

We were right. He came through here. And he left me a sign.

My chest is still tugging. Maybe it's the tin-can-telephone string. Maybe it's something else. Mari catches up with me, her eyes flicking from me to the little stone tower and back again.

"What's that?" she asks.

"A trail marker."

I stumble to tell her about them. About our trail marker system. About the way Joel and me used them in our Woodland Elves game. About the arrow made of sticks I thought I saw back when we first set out this morning. Even after all this time, after everything we've been through together, part of me worries that I'm talking too much. That I'm showing Mari too much of our weird. But the more I talk, the more and more lit up Mari's eyes get.

"You were right." She's running her fingers through her purple-streaked bangs like she just needs something to do with her hands. "I mean, I didn't doubt it, but—this—you—" She gives a breathless little laugh. "He was here, then."

I nod. "He was here."

We both just stand there, listening to the bird calls and the flowing river. I love this place. I love the quiet. I love the sunlight that streams through the tree branches and warms my face. I love the places where it paints golden spots on the ground.

I don't understand how I can feel so tied to this place—to the trees and the woods and the whispering river—and still have a lurking suspicion that I don't quite fit and never will. How I can feel like the woods are a part of me, and yet I want to run and run until I'm someplace, anyplace, else.

I don't want to be here, I think, but that's not really true.

Maybe what's truer is this: *I don't want to be me.*

There's a glint of sunlight reflecting off the ground beside the stone mound. Something's tucked into a knot of grass beside the bottom rock.

I crouch to pick it up.

Joel's pocketknife. The one his dad gave him when he turned twelve. The blade's pulled out—that's what caught the light. It's all sharp metal and dangerous angles. I'm afraid to fold it back into the handle. Whenever Joel's tried to close it, it always gets a little bit stuck and makes me worry he's going to cut off a finger.

Mari's voice over my shoulder has gone soft when she says, "Is that his?"

"Yeah." I show her the initials carved into the side: *JG*. Joel Gallagher. "He must've dropped it."

I've never looked at the initials on the knife too closely. I always just figured Joel's dad had gotten it monogrammed for him before he wrapped it up for Joel's birthday last year. But now, it's obvious the initials were carved in by hand. Scratched in with a blade. Did Joel do that? I'm trying to work out how he could've used the knife to carve the handle—he must've done it with a second knife, I guess—when I realize suddenly that *JG* aren't just Joel's initials. They're his dad's initials, too. Jonathan Gallagher.

I'd bet almost anything that Joel didn't carve

those. I'd bet almost anything that his dad did, years ago, when the knife was his. And that when Joel was old enough—when he'd decided that Joel *should* be old enough to want this kind of thing—Jonathan passed it on.

Joel's dad has been trying to get Joel to act "right" for as long as I've known Joel. He stuck Joel on the church peewee baseball team when we were in first grade. Joel got put in left field and spent the whole season collecting wildflowers and funny-shaped rocks from the grass in the outfield. He signed Joel up for Cub Scouts for a while, too. Joel went to the meetings for a year. After each one, he'd come back and complain to me about how much he hated Cub Scouts.

His dad had his idea of Joel, and he was trying to stamp that on top of the *actual* Joel, and it didn't work. The actual Joel just kept slipping through.

"Should we take it with us?" Mari asks.

I turn the pocketknife over and over in my hand. The hinge has a little mud caked into the grooves from getting left in the dirt.

And maybe because Joel is somewhere else on the river, too, maybe because the water's connecting us, I *do* feel him. It's like I catch one of his feelings: *This is what he felt.* And it hits me that Joel didn't forget his pocketknife here.

He got rid of it. On purpose.

Joel and I have always played in the woods, where we can pretend to be anybody we want.

Maybe Joel left because he was tired of other people trying to tell him what kind of person he was supposed to be. His dad, or Rudy Thomas, or anybody in Riverview. Maybe he left because he was deciding who he was.

I remember a point from earlier this year, or maybe lots of points all blending together in my memory. Just a feeling. Playing in the woods with Joel. Leaves overhead, dirt underfoot. Warm breeze on my face. And for a moment, it hit me that, while Joel and me were playing, I felt like myself.

And that was when I realized just how much I'd been watching myself from the outside. When I realized that watching from the outside had become my normal. Just drifting along behind myself, seeing me the way everybody else did, but knowing that their view didn't match up with how *I* saw me, from the inside. Feeling frustrated at the difference.

Maybe you can't really, truly tell how bad things are till you get a moment when they're not.

PIECES

I STARE OUT OVER THE WATER, AND MY BRAIN IS SWIRLING WITH PIECES from all over the place, pieces that don't quite make sense.

A piece: Sometime maybe a year or two back, riding in the car with my mom. She's listening to a talk-radio program on NPR, and the host is interviewing someone who everyone used to think was a boy but she isn't, really. She's transgender. A trans woman. Everyone thought she was a boy when she was born, she says, but they got it wrong.

Sometimes they get it wrong.

A piece: Earlier this year, Joel and me hanging

out at Mari's house, eating cheese and crackers at their kitchen table. Mama Callie and Mama Elena are talking about a friend of theirs who just visited from Asheville. They show us a picture stuck to the fridge with a magnet. Short hair and sharp eyebrows and a leather jacket with patches sewn onto it.

"I like her jacket," Joel says. He looks closer at the picture. "Or, sorry—*his* jacket?"

Mama Callie and Mama Elena lock eyes for a second over all our heads. "Bell isn't really a 'he' or 'she' kind of person," Mama Elena says. "Just a person. We just call them by their name or by 'they' instead of 'he' or 'she.'" She smiles. "But yes, their jacket is pretty dope."

A piece: A flutter in my stomach. A feeling like I'm close to something but I'm afraid to touch it. When the woman on NPR starts explaining what *transgender* means, my mom changes the station over to Christian rock.

"We don't need *that*," she murmurs, and I think it's to herself, not to me, but I drop my head against the car window. Let the bumps from the road rattle through my skull.

At Mari's house, Mama Elena and Mama Callie keep talking about the visit with their friend. The friend who's not a "he" or "she" kind of person. I chew my cracker and stare down at my lap, digging my fingernails into the palms of my hands. I don't want anyone to see me.

A piece: Realizing that I've felt like there's something wrong with me for a long while. I've wanted to hide because that seemed less scary than letting other people know the parts of me that feel secret.

A piece: Realizing that maybe I'm not the only one.

THE COPPERHEAD

"YOU OKAY?" MARI SAYS, PEERING AT MY FACE, AND FOR A TERRIFYING second I think she can see it all right there. All right there in the open.

"I'm fine," I say. "We should go."

"Should we take the knife with us?" she asks again. "To give it back to him when we find him?"

I just shake my head. Let her words slowly pull me back into myself. *When we find him.* Not *if*, but *when*. That's what I hang on to.

I use the flat of my palm to push the pocketknife blade back inside, and snap the knife shut.

I tuck it back into the grass beside the mound of stones. Mari just nods.

She checks the map on her phone again, and we continue on, following the river farther south and a little west. My feet are starting to ache. How far have we walked today already? Ten miles? Fifteen? Teagan will have found Joel's mom by now. They'll both be out looking for us. Teagan probably called our parents at work, and our parents will be driving out here to track us down, and the police will probably have gotten involved, too. Officer McCarthy and the sheriff in Calumet and all the other sheriffs in all the other nearby counties. It's the same people who Officer McCarthy have out watching for Joel. Everything is closing in, closing in.

Two days ago, my dad was telling me he was proud of me. He won't be proud of me anymore. Not when he finds out about all the lies I've told. Not when he finds out I set a fire in a church, even if it was an accident. We're out in the fresh forest air, but my breath keeps getting stuck in my throat.

Maybe it's the humidity.

"We can cut over again once the river bends back up," Mari is saying, still studying her map. "Once we round this tip to the south. See? And then we can just keep heading west. Unless you've got any more brilliant insights about where Joel would've stopped. I can't believe he left you a rock pile as a sign and you *found* it. Along this whole length of river." She waves a hand at the river ahead of us. "Seriously, it's freaky how well you two—*Watch out!*"

She yelps the last part, and I about jump out of my skin. I'd probably land right on the thing she told me to watch out for, except that Mari grabs my arm from midair and yanks me backward. We both go tumbling back against a tree, and all I'm seeing is sky, leaves, Mari's flailing limbs.

"What?" I'm babbling. "What? What?"

"There!"

She's pointing wildly at the underbrush where we were just walking. It takes my eyes a second to focus.

But then I see it. Coiled in the grass. Shimmering and scaly and still.

The snake raises its head, very slowly, and studies us. Its scales are shiny and brown, with darker brown bands running down its length, and it glints in the sunlight. With every movement, its muscles flex visibly under the skin, looking sleek and powerful.

Mari and me have both gone very, very still.

There are tons of different snakes in Kentucky, although Joel and I have never found many in our woods. Once, when we were in elementary school, we saw a big king snake with black scales slithering up the hill beside the Sacred Spot. More often, we've spotted garter snakes, so skinny and well camouflaged that we can only see them when they skitter across the path in front of us.

But in our part of the state, there are only two kinds of snakes that are venomous: rattlesnakes and copperheads.

Rattlesnakes are easy to recognize. You don't have to bother studying their bands or the shapes of their heads to identify them—you just have to look for the rattle on their tails. Just like in the movies. They warn you out of their space.

Copperheads are trickier. They don't have a warning system. They'll lurk in the underbrush until they can't lurk anymore. Even if they don't *want* to bite you, they'll do it if they feel like they're in danger. They'll do it if you get too close. One of my field guides had a diagram for how to recognize a copperhead, but my brain's turned blank. All I can remember is to look for just what the name says.

The snake that's gazing up at me and Mari has a smooth, copper-colored head.

"Back away slow," I say quietly, even though I can't make myself move. I can feel my own pulse pounding in my head and my chest and the palms of my clenched hands. My heartbeat is fast and alive. Marking the seconds as we stare at the copperhead, and the copperhead stares at us.

"Is it venomous?" Mari breathes.

"Yeah."

Mari's hand slips into mine. Hers is warm and a little sweaty.

"We've gotta go," she says.

I still can't move, though. It's like I'm stuck, just staring at all these possibilities. The ways everything could change all at once with just one wrong move. This snake could slither forward too fast for me to react and plunge its fangs right through my sock, into my ankle. Joel's raft could already have flipped over, or the blue rain barrels could've sprung a leak, or he could be lost or scared or in danger anywhere out here along the river. And me, this thing inside me...It could change everything.

Then the snake twitches toward us—

Mari and me both scream—full-on bloodcurdling screams that cut through the quiet of the woods. I don't remember turning to run, but we're running again, or maybe it's more like stumbling, lurching through the underbrush. We leave the river far behind. I have no idea where we're heading. I wish we had a trail, wish we had some kind of path to follow instead of just staggering through leaves and vines and unknown. The farther we go, the more treacherous and uncertain every single step I take feels.

I keep imagining I see another copperhead springing out of the brush. My heart is clenched up tight.

But Mari's hand is still in mine, tugging me along, and so I just cling to that. We're running, and then we're slowing down, slow enough that we can talk through our panic and our gasping breaths. "We're okay," Mari is saying, even as we keep stumbling along. "We're okay, we're okay."

"We're okay," I agree. But it feels like a lie.

At last Mari's hand slips out of mine, and I rub my sweaty palms. The forest around us is both unfamiliar and familiar at the same time. Trees that I know, smells that I know. But it's not the safe woods I've always known. It's not the safe hug of Riverview, where I can play safe pretend games with Joel and then go home. This is somewhere new and strange.

"Maybe we should stop," I say.

Mari's footsteps slow. "To catch our breath?" she says. "Yeah. I could use that." She doubles over for a minute, breathing hard, and starts rummaging through my backpack for a water bottle. She pulls out two granola bars and passes one to me.

"No, I mean…maybe we should stop this. Go back."

Mari stares at me.

We've paused beside a huge oak tree, bigger and thicker than the ones around it. A pin oak, I think.

Almost as thick as the bur oak that leans over Mystic Creek. I sink back against the trunk of it, pressing my palms into the rough bark. The tree is something solid to hang on to, at least. I can't look at Mari, so I look down at my fingers running up and down the ridges in the bark.

"Maybe Teagan was right," I hear myself saying. "This is dangerous, and we don't know what we're doing, and we could've just got bit by a snake, and I dragged you into all of this and—"

"You didn't drag me into anything," Mari says. "I knew what I was getting into."

A butterfly lands on the tree by my hand, wings flickering orange and black. A monarch. I watch it take off for a second and then land again. It stretches its wings.

"Do *you* want to keep going?" Mari asks finally.

The honest answer is I'm scared. The honest answer is I think we're hitting a point of no return, and not just because our parents and the police are probably out looking for us and we'll get in trouble if we go back. The honest answer is I don't know how this is going to end.

I don't know if I can unthink these pieces inside me, now that I've let myself think them. They're terrifying.

So maybe it's not lying when I take a deep breath and square up my shoulders. "Yeah," I say. "I want to keep going."

THE LAST DAY OF SCHOOL

MARI AND ME SET OUR COURSE WEST, ANGLING OUR ROUTE SO WE'RE between the river to the north of us and the highway to the south. I don't think I've ever walked this far in my life. The bottoms of my feet twinge with every step, almost like they're bruised, and I'm growing blisters where my sneakers rub against my pinky toes.

"Where did you and Joel get the idea for those trail markers?" Mari asks as we walk.

"A hiking book," I say.

"You read a lot of hiking books, right? And nature books?"

"And field guides."

"So you must know a ton about all the different plants and animals around here, right? Like, what's that one?" She nods at a thick-trunked tree on our right.

"Ash, I think," I say. And because she's still watching me, still waiting, I keep talking. I tell her about all the different trees we're passing, and about the ways you can figure out what kind they are. I tell her about simple and compound leaves and what you can tell by the way they're positioned on a branch. I tell her about how to count a leaf's lobes.

She doesn't roll her eyes at me or laugh or zone out, and the longer I talk, the less I think about it. The less I have to worry about saying the right thing. Mari just listens. She asks questions. She spots a woodpecker high above us and asks me about it. She tells me about the little tree in the backyard of her old house in North Carolina.

"A dogwood," she says. "I don't know very many kinds of trees, but I know that one."

"I bet it was beautiful in the spring," I say.

"Yeah." She smiles, and her face is a little far away, but not because she's bored. "It always bloomed this really pale pink. And all the petals would drop and make the whole yard pink, too."

I remember asking Mari once if she liked it in Riverview. If she was glad her moms had moved here and left North Carolina. It was back in the fall, before the Running-Away Game had started but after Mari had joined Joel's and my lunch table. That day, we'd finished the worksheet Mrs. Littlewood had given us, and Mari had turned around in her chair to face me. She was drumming her fingers on the edge of my desk. Her fingernails were painted purple, just like her hair, but the paint had chipped in some places.

"Do you miss where you used to live?" I asked.

She'd been asking me questions for weeks, but I hadn't really asked much of anything about her. Usually I just kind of let her fill in the empty spaces. Most of the time she didn't wait to be asked stuff— she just told me. I knew she and her moms had moved back to take care of her grandma, who was getting sick. I knew they'd lived in Asheville before.

"Of course I miss it," she told me then. Almost too fast. Her fingers had stopped drumming, but her pointer finger still rested there on the edge of my desk, the only thing holding her hand up over her lap. "I mean, I get why we had to come here. But it was just...bigger there. You know?"

I didn't know. I've never lived anywhere but Riverview; I don't know how anyplace else compares.

"Do you like it here, though?" I asked.

"Hmm," Mari said.

And then the bell rang, and we both picked up our books, and I never asked her again. I guess I didn't want to hear the answer. I was afraid that if I asked again if Mari liked Riverview, she'd announce that she hated it, and she hated Joel and me, and she wanted to leave. She wanted out.

Which is funny, because Joel and me obviously wanted out, too.

As we talk, I have a sneaking feeling Mari knows what it's like to want to run away, too. Just like Joel. Just like me. Maybe it's why I'm glad to have her here with me, even while I'm glad we haven't told my parents or Joel's parents or anybody else. Maybe it's why she agreed to come along.

We keep walking for ages, stopping for only a few minutes at a time. We check our location on Mari's phone, tracking our progress as our little blue dot moves farther along the river's course. We eat more snacks and drink from our water bottles, and a couple of times, we have to duck behind trees to use the bathroom.

But we never stop for long. Every time we pause, it's harder than ever to make my feet start moving again. And that's after only a short break. If we sit down, I worry I won't be able to stand up again.

It's the middle of the afternoon by the time we cross over into Mammoth Cave National Park. I wouldn't be able to tell that we're in the park at all, except that its borders are marked on the map on Mari's phone. We can see right when our little blue dot moves inside it. The sun's pounding down overhead and the humidity is stifling, but the canopy of trees protects us from the worst of the heat.

"Was that the whole story?" Mari asks suddenly.

"What story?" I say.

"About what happened the night Joel disa—the night he left. The story you told everyone. It just feels like it's missing parts."

"What's missing?"

I don't know why I'm playing dumb. Obviously there are parts missing. And obviously, by now, Mari can tell.

"You tell me," she says. "I mean, I didn't know about the raft till this morning. I knew you two kept leaving school, and I knew you were up to *something*, but I didn't know…" She's frowning a little now, a line between her dark eyebrows. A line like the one Joel likes to point out on *my* face when I'm worried about something. "I don't know. There's obviously stuff you were keeping to yourself. Which is fine—I get it."

I feel like there's a rock stuck in my throat again. I try to swallow it down.

"Well, you know what happened earlier that day," I say finally. "Last day of school."

Mari goes quiet. We're both remembering it. Rudy Thomas had taken Joel's sneakers at the end of PE, as we were all changing back out of our gym clothes for the last time of the year. He'd snatched them and taken off running around the gym while Joel chased him in his socked feet, and everybody watching acted like they were both just goofing around, even though, with Rudy Thomas, it was never *just* goofing around. Rudy Thomas had smirked, and then he'd thrown Joel's sneakers through the open doorway of the girls' locker room. They'd bounced into the cobwebby corner behind the benches.

"Yeah," Mari says.

"And you know what happened after."

"Yeah."

I don't mean right after, when I waited till the bell rang and Rudy Thomas had left the gym before I went into the girls' locker room to get Joel's shoes for him—I felt like an intruder in there, too, but at least it was empty. I don't mean when Joel sat on the empty bleachers and tied them, neither of us saying a word.

I mean the part Mari was there for. At lunch, when she heard about what'd happened, she insisted on going to Vice Principal McDonnell's office. Joel and me had both given up ages before that; we both knew that the teachers and McDonnell weren't going to do a single thing about Rudy Thomas being Rudy Thomas. But Mari had said, "Come on, it's the end of the year. What have you got to lose?"

"She could end up calling my parents," Joel had said.

"And that'd be a bad thing?"

Joel shrugged. "Depends on which of them she gets."

But he'd gone quiet for a while, his Thinking face. And he'd decided to go to McDonnell's office after all. I don't know what was different about that time. Maybe he was thinking of our almost-finished raft hooked to the bur oak tree deep in our woods. Maybe Mari's anger on his behalf convinced him. We all three went to McDonnell's office together.

Mari led the way. She told the whole story to McDonnell. About the shoes in the locker room. About the things Rudy Thomas had said. *Just go get 'em, Gallagher. Go in your locker room and get 'em.* She even told McDonnell about the other word Rudy Thomas had called Joel, although her voice shook a little bit as she said it.

As Mari was retelling it, Joel just stared at the floor. Quieter than he ever is. I reached over to where one of his hands was clutching the chair's armrest, and I wrapped my hand overtop it.

After Mari finished the story, Vice Principal McDonnell folded her hands across the desk. For just one moment, I thought she was going to actually make something happen. Like Rudy Thomas might actually get in trouble.

"I'm very sorry you had a bad experience today, Mr. Gallagher," she said. She was looking down her nose at Joel, peering over the edge of her glasses, like she didn't want to get too close.

"It wasn't just today," Mari said. "He's been doing this all year."

"I'll talk to Coach Nielsen about the incident. In the meantime, you all should return to your classes. Mrs. Danson can write notes for your teachers about why you're late."

In the meantime. They were waiting us out, I realized. Just counting down the time till the day ended and sixth grade was officially over and they wouldn't have to deal with us again till next year.

When there'd be nothing to stop all this from happening all over again.

"That's not good enough," Mari said. Like she'd read my mind. Like she could feel my frustration, simmering slowly to a boil under my skin, except that as much as I wanted to I couldn't find my voice to say anything. Mari spoke up without a second thought.

McDonnell's eyebrows were climbing slowly upward. "I'll be calling Mr. Thomas down to talk to him in a few minutes," she said slowly. "However, you should return to class before I have to give *you* a talking-to as well, Miss Clark-Espinoza."

Like the two things were just the same. Like Rudy Thomas calling Joel that word and Mari talking back to an adult to stand up for Joel were equally bad.

Joel was already standing. He gave my hand a tug, and then Mari's, and we filed out of the office and over to Mrs. Danson's desk for our tardy notes.

"I'm sorry," Mari said softly. "I really thought—"

"It's whatever," Joel said before she could finish. He grinned his Cover-Up Smile. "Two more classes till summer, right?"

As Mrs. Danson asked us our teachers' names, I could hear McDonnell on the phone in her office. Talking to Coach Nielsen, I guessed. I wondered if Coach Nielsen even knew what had happened during his class. He'd been in the gym for the whole thing. But he hadn't said a word.

"Something that happened last period," McDonnell was saying on the phone. "With two of your students..."

"I'll just write one note for you two together," Mrs. Danson told Joel and me. "Since you're in the same class. Saves me paper."

"Yes, I know," McDonnell's voice said. Through the window, she was shaking her head. "*Yes*, I know. No, I don't think we need to—I understand. I'll be talking to Mr. Thomas. No, I don't think we'll need to get parents involved at this point."

There was a long pause.

Mrs. Danson held out our tardy slips. "You're all set," she said.

"I know," McDonnell was saying into the phone. "Poor kid. But honestly, I'm not sure what he expects."

Joel heard her loud and clear. I knew he did. His face was blank, an empty hole.

As we headed back into the hallway and toward our next classes, those were the words that kept hovering right behind us. *Poor kid. I'm not sure what he expects.* The *poor kid* wasn't Rudy Thomas. The *poor kid* was Joel. Joel, who was pulling the Cover-Up look back over his face, tucking away everything that had happened. Joel, who was now telling Mari about a new episode of some TV show neither of us knew but that Joel swore was the funniest show he'd ever seen.

Honestly, I'm not sure what he expects.

Like McDonnell couldn't, or wouldn't, do anything about it. Like there was nothing *to* do. Like Rudy Thomas saying those things is just the way things go because of who Joel is: because he's goofy and different and Black, because he's willing to do what he wants and like what he likes without worrying about what other people think. Like this is just what Joel gets for being who he is in a place where people don't want him to be.

A DIFFERENT CONFESSION

"WAS THAT WHAT DID IT?" MARI ASKS NOW. "DID HE TELL YOU THAT'S WHY he was leaving?"

"He didn't tell me he was leaving at all," I say.

But it's not exactly true. I'm remembering Joel from that night by the campfire: *Listen, my mom's been talking about going away for a while....* It's a blur of hurt and anger and fear, tumbling into a sinkhole and never hitting the bottom. Stuck in the falling.

"But I mean, did he talk about it more that night?" Mari says. "I know he didn't want to talk about it at school. But it seemed like...well, like it was probably a big part of the reason."

I think about that night. When Joel both did and didn't talk about what happened at school that day. When he wouldn't quite use the words, but he talked *around* it enough that it formed a perfect outline. I think about the desperate look on Joel's face, and about what he told me, and how I reacted, and what he had tried to do, and about our parents' two-tents rule, and a prickly feeling starts filling me up, pins and needles that happen sometimes when I feel both too stuck inside my own body and like I've never actually been inside my own body in the first place.

Finally I just say, "Yeah."

"And all that stuff that'd been happening at school. It was part of why you both started sneaking out in the first place, right? Why you and Joel started building the raft?"

"Yeah."

That line is there between Mari's eyebrows again. It makes my stomach ache thinking about how Joel left me behind. But Joel and me did the same thing to Mari first. When we ran off over the science annex fence that day without a second thought. When we kept doing it. When we decided without ever really deciding that it had to stay a secret—even from Mari. Joel and me were so caught up in getting ourselves away that we didn't even think to ask Mari if she needed to get away, too.

Up ahead of us, through the trees, a movement catches my eye. A car. We've found the road again. That's easier to focus on than the hollowed-out, guilty feeling in my chest, so I say, "Hey, the road," and start at a jog toward it.

I don't really expect Mari to follow me. But after a couple of seconds, I hear her footsteps behind me. She does.

We're only twenty yards or so from the car when I realize what it is.

"Down," I hiss. "Get down!"

My stomach feels like it's dropped already, and it's easy for the rest of me to drop to the ground, too. I scramble for Mari's arm till she flattens herself in the dirt beside me. I end up with a leaf in my mouth somehow, but I don't dare move to spit it out. It tastes bitter, or maybe that's just the panic.

The vehicle on the road is a ranger's truck: white

and green, with U.S. PARK RANGER stamped across the side and big police lights stuck on top. The hazard lights on the truck's front and back are flashing, but not the lights on top—not yet, at least. The truck drives along the road slow, so slow, and we're close enough that through the underbrush I can see the driver peering back and forth as they inch along, scanning the woods on either side. Looking for something.

Or someone.

"Us?" Mari breathes. "Do you think they're looking for us?"

"Maybe." But in my mind, it's more than a maybe. It's a definitely. Teagan told, and Joel's mom told, and unlike with Joel, they both knew the direction we had come from and the direction we were going. Now they've got the authorities out driving around searching for us.

We're officially in hiding. We're officially on the run.

The truck slows even more, and for a moment it stops. The ranger in the driver's seat leans out through the open window, squinting in the distance. For a second, I swear their eyes land right on us.

I press my face flat to the dirt and squint my eyes shut, but that gaze still burns on the back of my neck. My heart's thudding so hard it hurts, and a branch is poking into my stomach, and in the dark behind my closed eyelids it's too easy to imagine another copperhead slithering out of the brush toward us.

Finally I hear the truck's tires start forward again, crunching along the road. Mari lets out a little huff of air beside me—she'd been holding her breath. I risk a peek up through the leaves in time to see the truck's taillights disappearing around the bend.

We lie there for a long while, waiting for the truck to come back. But slowly, my muscles relax. Slowly, I can look over at Mari and see her looking back at me, our cheeks both pressed to the ground. She smiles a little at me.

"We're okay," she says.

But up close, I can see the little line between her eyebrows still. That little crease of uncertainty on her face.

I push myself into sitting up. Mari does the same.

"We should've told you," I say softly.

She blinks at me. "What?"

"When Joel and me left school. I wasn't thinking. Well, maybe I was, but I don't know *what* I thought. And now you've been out here all day helping find him, and helping *me*, and hiding out, and—we should've told you. It wasn't fair that we didn't."

It's the kind of confession that feels better for having said it, even though it feels worse at the same time. This confession *is* admitting guilt. It's realizing I messed up, and there's not a way to put things back.

"I do really wish you'd told me," Mari says.

"I'm sorry."

After you confess your sins in church, after you've listed off everything you've done wrong to the priest in the sacrament of confession, the priest gives you a penance to do. Something to do to start to make up for your sins. Sometimes the penance is praying: He'll have you say a certain number of Hail Marys or Our Fathers. Other times he'll tell you to read a certain chapter of the Bible or to do a good deed for someone. Even after the priest says the finishing prayer and tells you God's forgiven your sins, you aren't done—you have to go actually say the prayers, or read the chapter, or do the good deed. You have to put in the work to make things better. You have to try your best not to do the same sins again.

Confessing to people isn't so different, I guess. Even after you say you're sorry, you still have to put in the work to fix what you've done. It doesn't just go away.

"I don't think the truck is coming back," Mari says finally. "We should move away from the road."

She pushes herself to her knees and offers me a hand, too. We brush ourselves off and then head back the way we came, deeper into the woods. We move doubled over, hunched and hiding like spies or like Woodland Elves scouting through enemy territory.

When the road's well out of sight behind us, we stop to check Mari's map. My stomach's started rumbling like nobody's business, so we pick out a soft patch of moss to sit on so we can eat. It's that weird time between lunch and dinner, but we never stopped for a real lunch, and my meals are all messed up. I dig out bread and peanut butter and a plastic knife, and we make ourselves peanut butter sandwiches and eat them surrounded by birdcalls and pretend that everything's okay.

"I wish I'd gone camping with y'all that night," Mari says out of nowhere.

"Me too." I wish that for a lot of reasons.

"It would've been better than Louisville, anyway." She takes a deep breath, and I realize suddenly that this is a confession of her own. "My moms are making me see a therapist," she says. "For anxiety and stuff. There's one in Louisville who specializes in working with kids with gay parents."

"Oh," I say. I haven't been a very good friend at all. All this while, I've been waiting for Mari to pack up and leave, to realize that she's too good for Joel and me. But she needed us. She needed us as much as we needed her.

And I just wasn't paying enough attention to notice.

I don't know what's the right thing to say. "Are you okay?" I ask.

"Yeah. I mean, therapy's hard work. But I guess it's helpful. I started getting anxiety attacks, and I guess it's gotten better since I've talked to somebody. And I know my moms worry. And I know they feel guilty. It's just...harder here. You know?"

I've never lived anywhere else, so I *don't* know. I

just kind of nod, and I wait, and that's enough for her to keep going.

"I get why my mom made us move here," Mari says. "But everything was *easier* in Asheville. It wasn't perfect, but it was easier. There were just… more different kinds of people there. And we had a community. Here, I feel like my moms just spend all their time bracing themselves, always having to be prepared that some homophobe's going to say something, or do something, and so *I'm* bracing myself, too, and it's just exhausting. Feeling like you're never quite going to fit in, you know? Feeling like you're always on the outside. I just—"

She stops herself, like she thinks she's said too much. But I do know. I really do.

"But it's fine," she finishes. "It's whatever."

It isn't whatever. I can tell by the way Mari is looking carefully at her hands but stealing glances every so often at me, trying to see how I'm reacting. I can tell by the way her voice sounds almost perfectly casual, except for a little shake in her breathing. I notice these things because I've done them, too.

They're things that happen sometimes when

you've been holding on to a secret. When you *are* a secret. When you've figured there are thoughts you have in your brain or pieces of who you are that you'll never be able to share with anyone.

They're things that happen when you decide to share those parts anyway.

Maybe Mari has sandstone and limestone layers, too, just like the layers that make up Mammoth Cave here underneath our feet. Just like me. Maybe she has caverns of secrets carving through the limestone, miles and miles, covered up and protected by the sandstone surface. Maybe everyone does.

I still don't know what's the right thing to say or do—should I say something comforting? Give her a hug? Tell her everything is going to be okay? None of that feels right. I wipe the peanut butter off my hands, and then I lean over in the grass and bump my shoulder against hers, just a little bit. She looks over at me and smiles. Lets out a little laugh. She bumps my arm back, and then she brushes the back of her hand against the back of my hand, and I loop my fingers into hers. Both our hands are kind of sweaty.

"Slimy," Mari says, and I laugh.

"I know I'm not great at talking," I say. "But I'm here, okay? Whatever you need. I'm here for it."

"Okay," she says.

I'm still thinking about Joel and me at our campsite that night, when my own hurt got in the way of seeing that Joel was hurting, too. When I got so caught on how I needed him that I couldn't understand, or didn't *want* to understand, that he needed something else.

We have to find him. *I* have to find him, and soon, because I have so many things to say to him, starting with this: *I'm sorry.*

"Ready to keep going?" I say, brushing bread crumbs off my shorts and pushing the peanut-buttery knife back into the backpack. I pull Mari to her feet.

And that's where we are when the park ranger spots us.

RANGER SANDRA

"HEY!" THE PARK RANGER CALLS. "YOU CAN'T PICNIC OUT HERE! ARE Y'ALL lost?"

My first instinct is to run. We've been running all day. Running into the woods. Running away from the church in Calumet. Running away from my sister. The park ranger isn't the same one from the truck. She's dressed all in green and brown—green slacks, brown button-down shirt, brown brimmed hat with a green band wrapped around it. She must've come from some ranger station or other, but for a second it doesn't feel that way. It feels like she sprang straight out of the trees. And so it feels like there's nowhere *to* run, because the only thing around us is more trees.

I want to hide again, to flatten myself on the ground. But it's too late. We've already been spotted. All we can hope now is that this ranger isn't one of the ones searching for us.

Mari is watching me, probably waiting for me to take the lead, but I'm frozen.

"Uh, kind of lost, yeah," she calls back.

"Trail's over here," the park ranger says. "Don't—" She winces as we start toward her. "Don't step on anything."

It's impossible to not step on *anything*. I want to tell the ranger that I know why it's bad to hike off the trails, but maybe that makes it even worse that we did it anyway. Mari and I try our best to place our sneakers on the emptiest spots we can as we pick our way toward her. Sure enough, where the ranger's standing, the underbrush clears out in a long path of dirt and gravel. The trail winds off over the hills.

"Thanks," Mari says, because my voice is still frozen.

"Hold up," the park ranger says. She's got a patch sewn on her shirt that reads *Sandra*. It's sewn right underneath her golden ranger badge. "Who're you two out here with?"

"Uh," Mari says. She glances at me again. "No one. Just us."

"How'd you wind up off the trail?"

"We just got lost."

"Stay on the trail and you won't *get* lost," Ranger Sandra says. "We have trails for a reason. Besides, hiking out there hurts the local ecosystem."

"I know," I say. "Sorry."

Ranger Sandra is squinting at us. Her hat brim makes the top of her face shadowy.

"Okay, thanks," I say, ducking away and grabbing for Mari's hand again. I start to pull her along the path. "We'll stick to the trail from here on out."

"Wait a second." When I don't wait, she grabs the top handle of my backpack, locking me in place. "You two from over in Riverview, by any chance?"

And that's it. We're caught. We're done.

Ranger Sandra marches us back along the trail like the general of the elvish army marching prisoners of war. Like the bad guy in our Secret Agents game marching away his hostages. Like the pirate captain getting ready to make us walk the plank.

She makes us go ahead of her on the path, never letting me farther than an arm's reach away from her. She calls over to the park visitor center from the radio on her belt while we hike. "Remember those kids they were looking for from that church in Calumet? Well, guess who I just found wandering around in the park."

The crackly voice on the radio is shocked. It's impressed. It's getting in touch with Calumet law enforcement. We hear bits and pieces of the story of the afternoon in their conversation: Teagan stumbling back out of the woods into Calumet, telling Joel's mom and a very confused woman of the church that Mari and me were still out looking for Joel. Mrs. Gallagher contacting my parents and Mari's parents and Officer McCarthy back in Riverview. Officer McCarthy calling around to other police stations and ranger stations and anyone else in the area, putting everybody on alert to find us.

With every step, I feel like the ground's disappearing right under my feet. I feel like I'm going to sink straight through the earth.

"A," Mari whispers. It's the first time she's called me that instead of my full name. For a second, at least, I feel like I have something to grab on to. "I guess this is it, huh?"

This is as far as we go. And meanwhile, Joel is still out there, drifting on the river farther and farther away.

It's not supposed to end like this.

This isn't how the story is supposed to go.

RUDY THOMAS'S WORD

THE WORD RUDY THOMAS HAD CALLED JOEL AT THE END OF PE CLASS that last day of school started with an *f*.

He'd said it quietly, a mutter, but the shape of the word still came out like a punch. The drawled *a* after it, and then the harsh *g*'s and *t* of the second syllable. I would've known it was bad even if I didn't know what the word meant.

And I hadn't known, earlier in the year, when Rudy Thomas first started using it. I had to look it up. He said the word to Joel at lunchtime one day a couple of weeks into the year, and that afternoon, after school, I found the word in the huge unabridged dictionary my mom keeps in the den—the one that's almost a foot thick, bigger than the Bible. I was afraid to google a word that I instinctively knew was a swear.

The word Rudy Thomas had said is an offensive term for a person who's gay.

Gay was a word I already knew, even if I only knew it from bits and pieces. No one ever talked about it outright, at least not with me. I knew it from NPR segments on the radio in the car. I knew it from things kids at school whispered about Mari's moms. I knew it from throwaway lines Father Jacob tucked into the homilies at Mass sometimes, when he listed off *homosexuality* as one of many corruptions of the world, outside the straight and righteous path. *Homosexual* was Latin; I could decipher that one. *Homo-* meaning "same," *-sexual* meaning...well.

It was bad. I knew it was bad. I knew the word itself was bad because of the way Rudy Thomas hurled it, like something barbed and poisoned. And I knew what it meant was bad because everyone else just didn't talk about it at all.

Words like that are secrets. Or at least I figured that then.

We've all always known to keep them secret.

THAT NIGHT BY THE CAMPFIRE

THE NIGHT WE CAMPED IN THE WOODS, JOEL DIDN'T REPEAT THE WORD Rudy Thomas had said earlier in the day. The more Joel talked, though, the more the word hovered around him, poking holes through his sentences.

"He doesn't know what he's talking about," Joel said, breaking pieces off a dead tree branch and tossing them one by one into the fire. "I'm not a...I'm not that. He doesn't even know what..."

He'd run out of stick pieces to throw. He tangled his hands into the dark curls of his hair instead.

"I'm *not*," he said, without saying what he wasn't. "I'd know, right? I *can't* be."

"He doesn't know what he's talking about," I said, because we were so far out of what I knew how to talk about. I could only repeat Joel's own words back to him.

"I like girls, you know?" He sounded truly frantic now. "I *like*-like girls."

"I believe you," I said.

And I did. I believed him even as the words he said and the holes in his sentences made me feel like I was drifting away, like I was stuck inside my body but also floating away from it at the same time. A boat cut loose in the current. We weren't supposed to talk about this.

I did not want to talk about this.

After I'd looked up Rudy Thomas's word that first afternoon, I'd felt a panicky jolt in my stomach. I'd felt that panic during Father Jacob's homilies. And during those radio segments. I'd felt it every time someone around me had skirted close to talking about *gay* or *trans* but then hadn't, because if they won't even say those words outright, it means they're bad, right? Secrets are secrets for a reason, right? It's my mom and dad both pausing ever so slightly before they say "parents" when they're talking about Mari's two moms. It's my mom changing the radio station when the interview on NPR is with a woman who's trans, my mom murmuring to herself, "We don't need *that*."

There are things I don't know the rules for. That day in my mom's car, thoughts had skittered through my brain like the water droplets flicking across the car window. I knew better than to reach for them.

Everything I know about gay people or about trans people has come in bits and pieces. Because no one's told me outright.

I suddenly noticed that Joel wasn't looking at the campfire anymore. He was looking at me.

"I like *you*," he said then. "And you're a girl."

And I knew what he was going to say right before he said it, but there wasn't time to say anything, and I didn't know what to say anyway. I only knew that I felt very, very far away and the bungee cord holding me down had been cut loose and I didn't want to be there.

"Can I—can I kiss you?" he said.

"No!" I blurted out. We'd been sitting shoulder to shoulder all along, just like always, but suddenly the space between us felt too small. I scooted away without thinking. My skin was burning. "Just...no."

I didn't want to look at him, but I did anyway. His face had flickered into the Hurt look, just for a second, and then it switched into a different look that I didn't even have a name for.

"Sorry," he said. "I shouldn't have...sorry." And then, quieter, almost to himself, he said, "You don't believe me."

And I didn't know what to say. I didn't know how to tell him, *That's not what this is about. I believe you.*

I didn't know how to say, *You don't have to prove anything to me. I love you either way.*

I didn't know how to say, *I don't think you kissing me would mean what you think it means.*

There are so many times I wish I'd spoken up for Joel. I wish I'd asked him how to help. I wish I'd listened when he was trying to tell me what he needed.

I wish we'd talked, *really* talked—that we'd shared our secrets. I've been beating myself up for not noticing everything going on in his life, but he's missed what's going on in my life, too. We've both been so caught up in ourselves that we didn't even realize that maybe we could've been helping each other.

Because when Joel had said, "And *you're* a girl," I didn't know how to say, *Am I, though?*

Because I don't even know what that means. Being a girl is something that doesn't feel real to me. It feels like make-believe—like I'm putting on a role, but somehow even less real than our games of pretend in the woods. I don't know what being a girl means—not like my mom seems to know, or Teagan, or Joel's mom, or Mari, or even Mama Callie or Mama Elena.

It's not about the clothes or the hairstyles or painting my nails or shaving my legs. It's not about whether I know how to put on makeup or whether I want posters of boy bands on my bedroom walls like Teagan has or whether I want to talk with my friends about crushes at school.

No.

It's about finally learning to fit inside my own skin.

Like maybe I don't have to be a secret. Like maybe I don't have to keep a hard sandstone layer on top, hiding all the dark passages underneath. Like maybe what I feel on my inside is something I can say out loud, something I can let show on my outside, too.

WHAT OFFICER McCARTHY ALMOST SAID

WHEN I'M NOT SURE THE RIGHT THING TO SAY, IT'S SO MUCH EASIER TO just stay quiet. But there are so many times I should've said something, even if it didn't solve the problem. All those days when Rudy Thomas was bullying Joel, when I'd made a distraction but didn't confront him. On the last day of school, when Vice Principal McDonnell had said about Joel, *Honestly, I don't know what he expects*, like that was the best she could do.

And two days ago, when I was in Officer McCarthy's office answering questions. My dad was sitting beside me, fanning his face faster and faster with a brochure, his jaw clenched.

"We expect this sometimes," Officer McCarthy had said at the end of our meeting, as my dad and I got ready to leave. "From kids like him."

I didn't mean to say it, but the question slipped out of my mouth. "Kids like him?"

"Kids who're…" Officer McCarthy fumbled. He and my dad looked at each other over my head, and my dad's jaw clenched harder. Officer McCarthy seemed to rethink. "You know. Just twelve-year-old boys being boys. He'll turn up."

Afterward, I kept trying to figure out what Officer McCarthy had started to say. When he looked at Joel, what was he seeing? Did he think Joel was more likely to run away because he's Black? Did he think Joel was more likely to run away because he's a boy who doesn't act like boys are supposed to? If Joel being a "kid like him" had anything to do with why he ran away, it wasn't how Officer McCarthy had made it seem. It was because Joel was in Riverview. Because he lived in a mostly white town where he stands out from the crowd with just a glance. Because he lived in a place where people like his dad and Rudy

Thomas's dad want boys to act certain ways and like certain things.

And when Joel didn't fit, that town tried to squeeze him into place instead of letting Joel make the place fit *him*. They squeezed and squeezed until he couldn't stay anymore.

In Officer McCarthy's office, I waited for my dad to say something. I waited for him to make Officer McCarthy explain what he'd really meant or to tell him he was being racist.

My dad didn't say any of that. His teeth just stayed clamped together.

And so I didn't say anything, either.

THINGS I SHOULD'VE SAID

THE TRAIL RANGER SANDRA IS MARCHING US ALONG LEADS BACK TO THE road. She points us to a pickup truck parked on its edge, just like the truck we hid from earlier.

"In," she tells Mari and me.

The pickup doesn't have a back seat, so Mari and me hoist ourselves up and cram into the passenger side. I climb in first, so I have to fold my knees up to fit my feet on the hump in the middle of the floor. Mari buckles her seat belt on one side of me. Ranger Sandra climbs into the driver's seat on my other side and starts the truck.

We're squeezed in too tight. I wrap my arms up around my bare legs. Curl in on myself. Dirt from the woods has settled onto my sweaty skin in a thin layer of grime.

I don't want to be here.

But it's just a reflex. An automatic thought in my brain. I don't really mean it this time. I've spent so long just wanting to run away and leave everything behind and start over someplace no one knows me— feeling like that would be easier than dealing with whatever pieces are in front of me.

But I can't disappear now. I have too many things I need to say to Joel, things that are long overdue.

Ranger Sandra clunks the truck into gear, and we rumble down the road. Trees fly past the windows as we drive. This is the fastest Mari and me have moved all day—so much faster than walking. But it feels all wrong. Everything's tipped sideways.

There's one more piece from our fight that night. Joel's words are playing in my brain:

"Listen, my mom's been talking about going away for a while," Joel had told me by the campfire that night. "Getting out of Riverview. She's been talking about going to my aunt's in Louisville—her sister. I mean, they're always *talking* about it, but I think I'm gonna ask if we can finally—"

He stopped there, like he'd said too much. I'd heard the word, too. *We.* This wasn't just his mom talking about leaving. Joel was *asking* to go with her.

Joel wanted to go with her.

He was going to leave me.

That night, I'd just stood there. Sinking, sinking, sinking. He wasn't supposed to actually leave. I'd wanted out, wanted to leave Riverview, too, and the whole time we were playing the Running-Away Game I thought we both felt the same way about it—that it was a wild fantasy, a way to deal with that feeling of needing to be someplace else, but we wouldn't actually *do* it. It wouldn't actually fix anything. I was finally wrapping my head around the fact that there wasn't anywhere I could run away *to* that would fix what I felt, and I thought Joel would feel that, too— except that now, instead, Joel wanted to actually leave. For real.

I was too stuck in my own hurting to realize what

he was saying, to realize why he was telling me. He was telling me what he needed. He wanted me to understand. But I couldn't.

"Say something, Aubrey," he'd said.

I didn't say a single thing.

A REALIZATION

RANGER SANDRA FOLLOWS THE SIGNS TO THE VISITOR CENTER NEAR THE middle of the park. The visitor center is a huge golden-brick building. It's where tour groups meet up before going down into the cave. It's where the park rangers for our field trip every year have given us presentations about the cave ecosystem and the sandstone and limestone layers. It's just up the road from the cabins where my family and Joel's family camped a few years ago. The parking lot is bustling with cars and vans and school buses, families and rangers and camp groups.

After the quiet of the woods, it's all a little

overwhelming. Mari and me have been pulled back into the real world.

Ranger Sandra bypasses all the traffic and chaos in the main parking lot. She pulls over in a little side area by the visitor center's back entrance. She's been quiet as we drove. Letting us stew in our own thoughts. After she parks the truck, she just sits there for a minute. The engine clicks a little as it cools off.

"They'll have called your folks by now," she tells Mari and me. "They're gonna come pick you up. Can I just ask, though? What on *earth* were you two doing out in the middle of the woods?"

Mari looks at me. Her shoulder is still squeezed in against mine.

What were we doing?

What *are* we doing?

What are we going to do?

I don't know if I have answers to any of those.

When we don't say anything, Ranger Sandra sighs. She clicks off the safety lock on the door and gestures for us to get out of the truck. The sun is dipping lower in the sky, and our shadows on the pavement look like long-limbed aliens.

"Inside," Ranger Sandra tells us, holding open the visitor center's back door. The air-conditioning makes the sweat that's crusted onto my skin turn icy right away. She leads us down a brown linoleum hallway to a brown door that opens into a brown office with trail maps tacked to the walls. She settles us into brown chairs inside. "You can wait for your parents in here."

I hear the door lock behind her.

"What now?" Mari asks.

We still don't know where Joel is. Just that he's somewhere along the river. I remember the stick arrow in Riverview, and the stone mound we found. He's somewhere on the Green still, probably—but who knows? Maybe he's farther than that. Maybe he's already made it to the Ohio. Maybe he's heading down the Mississippi River by now. For all I know, he could be anywhere between Mystic Creek and the Gulf of Mexico.

He's still gone, and we're still here.

"What now?" Mari asks again.

And I don't know the answer. I just keep thinking

about Father Jacob at the vigil mass, calling Joel "our child," even though he'd never done anything before then to help Joel feel like he belonged here, just as he is. I keep thinking about Officer McCarthy organizing a search party and acting like he cares about Joel in front of the rest of the town, while privately telling us he expects this from "kids like him."

They've been lying, I know now.

But it's not always so obvious. There are so many lies of omission, too. It's my mom changing the radio when they say the word *trans*. It's so many things my parents never talk about, like if they pretend those things don't exist they'll just go away. It's all of our Cover-Up Smiles and clenched jaws and not speaking up because saying nothing is easier.

I haven't been the only liar in Riverview.

Mari has gotten too restless to sit in a chair. She's pacing back and forth across the linoleum. "Do you think my moms will understand?" she says. "They've been saying all year Joel needs people on his side, so maybe they won't be mad that we tried to go after him." She reaches the far wall of the office and swivels back around again. "Or maybe they'll ground me till I'm twenty-five."

"Mine will *definitely* ground me till then," I tell her.

She smiles now, just like she did when we made up the Running-Away Game. "We'll have to figure out some secret way to send messages to each other. Morse code, maybe."

"Homing pigeons," I suggest.

"Mounds of rocks left in the woods."

A huge trail map is tacked to the wall beside my chair, the paper curling a little at the edges. It shows the whole national park, with trails leading in almost every direction. I spot the visitor center, and close to it, the patch of cabins where our families camped. Just a little north of us, the blue line of the Green River winds through the heart of the park.

Without really thinking about it I trace my finger along the line. I trace from the easternmost edge of the map, where it flows down from Riverview, all the way to the other end, heading toward the Ohio. But something catches my eye.

Where the Green River passes beyond the far

border of Mammoth Cave National Park, a black line cuts across it.

"Dam," I say suddenly.

Mari blinks. "I think that's the first time I've heard you swear," she says.

But it wasn't a swear. "No. *Dam*." And I show her. The black line is just outside the park, over near Brownsville. The map marks it with red words: *Lock and Dam—must portage.*

The Brownsville Dam. The one my dad took me to see years ago. Folks have been talking about taking out the whole dam for ages, because it's cracked and ancient and leaks water.

The dam in Brownsville isn't enough to stop water from passing through. But it's enough to stop one boy and one raft.

Must portage.

My mind is racing, throwing piece after piece onto the pile. Would Joel be able to portage—would he be able to drag the raft over land by himself and push it back into the water? No way. Joel isn't athletic. We could barely pull the raft with both of us when we were building the thing. I'm impressed he even managed to get it into Mystic Creek by himself.

And he knows about the Brownsville Dam. He came with us that day when we stopped to see it on the way to Bowling Green. Joel would've figured out he couldn't make it beyond Brownsville on the river.

Which means that, if he's still with the raft, then he's still somewhere in Mammoth Cave National Park.

Just like that, it clicks in my head. It's like I've caught another of his feelings. Caught another of his memories, like when I found his knife and knew he'd thrown it away.

Except that this is one of my memories, too.

All day, Joel has been leaving me clues. Trail markers. Pointing me to him, just like in our Woodland Elves game. It's a place we've both been before. A place where the river curves, where one side turns into a rocky bluff. A place where the rocks open up into an entrance.

We'd promised to come back when we were older. *Just the two of us.*

"I know where he is," I say.

"What?" Mari says.

"I know exactly where to find him."

The office door bursts open. Mari and I both jump. Ranger Sandra stands in the doorway, her hands propped on her hips.

"Your families are here to pick you up," she says.

RECKONING TIME

"WHERE?" MARI WHISPERS TO ME AS RANGER SANDRA LEADS US OUT TO the lobby. "Where is he?"

But there's no time. Everything's crashing together.

Out by the information desk, my mom, my dad, Mama Callie, Mama Elena, and Teagan are all hovering in a clump. My mom is running her hands through her hair in the way she does when she's freaking out. Mama Callie and Mama Elena are both standing with their arms crossed, their heads craning around in every direction at once.

My dad spots us first, though. He locks eyes with me and doesn't even wait for Ranger Sandra to walk us over—he dodges around a camp group that's lining up to get back on their buses and rushes at us.

"Aubrey! Mari! Thank God you're okay!"

I've never heard my dad take the Lord's name in vain in my life. Maybe he's not taking it in vain, though. Maybe he's really thanking God. He scrunches me into one of those hugs that's so tight it hurts a little. One that pushes my face into his shirt. I'd braced myself for seeing them all, but somehow I still wasn't prepared for the *feeling* of it. I try to pick the right word for it: relief? Nerves? An adrenaline rush? It's some combination of all of them, and I'm glad I've got my face in his shirt, because my eyes are starting to prickle.

"I was so worried," he says, quiet, right in my ear.

Then my mom is hugging me, too, pressing me into a hug sandwich, and somewhere nearby Mari's moms are alternating between peppering her with relieved kisses and hissing out, "What were you *thinking*?"

Teagan is here, too. When my parents finally release me, she presses her hand into mine.

"I'm sorry," she says, and she gives my hand a little squeeze. "I had to."

"I know," I say.

That's when I see that my family and Mari's family didn't come alone. They've brought Joel's mom along, as well.

Her eyes are soft and a little sad. She's watching all of our hugs and happy reunions with a look on her face that Joel makes sometimes: one that's faraway and quiet and a little bittersweet.

Guilt washes over me fast and cold as the river. I've been telling myself we'd made the right choice, doing this on our own. But maybe it's not so simple.

Listen, my mom's been talking about going away for a while.

Joel's mom saw that Joel wasn't okay. She's been figuring out what to do to help him. Even if that meant going somewhere else. Even if that meant that she and Joel needed a new start—that they needed to go somewhere it would be easier. She hadn't done it quick enough, before Joel decided to leave on his own. But she was trying.

It was me. I was the one who didn't want them to leave. Who couldn't understand that what Joel needs and what I need are different things.

Leaving Riverview wouldn't solve whatever I need it to.

But it might be the right answer for Joel.

I peel myself out of the circle of my family and go to her. Look right in her eyes. "I'm really, really sorry," I say.

And I mean it. Not just because we got caught or are going to get in trouble. I'm sorry because she's hurting. She's been hurting since Joel left. She's been hurting since before that, probably. And instead of helping—instead of letting her help Joel—I messed it up.

She pulls me into a one-armed hug. "I'm so glad you're safe," she says. She doesn't have to say the second part for me to know what she's thinking: *I just hope he is, too.*

I have to finish this. I have to put this right.

TELLING THE PIECES

MARI, TEAGAN, AND ME END UP SETTLED ON A BENCH BY THE MAIN information desk while Ranger Sandra talks to our parents. Mari and me are the ones who've made all the trouble, but I'm guessing our parents have some questions to answer, too.

"I'm so sorry, A," Teagan says again when they're all out of earshot. "But I had to tell his mom. You get it, right? I had to get them to help. I didn't want to lose you, too."

"I get it," I say. And as betrayed as I felt when Teagan first said it in the woods, I really do. "I'm sorry we ditched you. That was, uh. Not cool."

"Not your best moment, but we're good," Teagan says. She wrinkles her mouth up into a smile. Something about the expression looks familiar—it's a face *I* make. It's one I've seen in photos of myself, or looking back at me in the mirror. We really do look a lot alike. Regardless of everything else—regardless of the other pieces—Teagan and me, we're siblings.

If all of us are liars in different ways, maybe the penance—the thing we can do to try to make it all okay—is this: We just keep working toward telling the truth. Telling it the best we can. Sometimes it doesn't have to be all at once. Sometimes we might not ever get there completely. The penance is in the trying.

I take a deep breath.

"So you know how they found that bungee cord in the woods?" I say. "On the tree by the river?"

I tell the whole story of what happened. The real version this time. I even tell the parts I haven't said outright to Mari—the parts I've been letting Mari piece together without ever actually saying. I say them this time.

"The raft was just supposed to be a game," I say.

275

"Just another way to distract Joel when things got bad. We weren't supposed to actually *use* it."

"Hmm," Teagan says.

"What's that mean? *Hmm*?"

"Just hmm," she says.

She's looking at me with her eyes a little pinched, a little thoughtful. Like she's seeing me in a new way. Like she's looking at her younger sibling and realizing I'm a person with my own life, too. I wonder if she knows that the raft wasn't *just* for Joel. That it was for me, too, in a different way.

For once, I don't shy away from Teagan studying me.

"I mean, it's dramatic," she says finally. "Building a whole raft and everything. Deciding to run away to who knows where. But I get the appeal." She leans back on the bench and kicks her feet out in front of her, her sneakers still muddy from hiking with us along the highway this morning. "Middle school sucks."

"Middle school seriously sucks," Mari says, kicking her feet out, too.

"Seriously," I say.

Mari jumps in to help tell the story where she

can. For the other parts, she leans her head against the wall and just listens. If she's mad about all the things Joel and I left her out of during those last two weeks of school, she doesn't show it. She's still here. She's helping me look for him anyway.

Finally I've caught them both up to the campfire that night. My stomach clenches just remembering it, but I tell it anyway.

"He wasn't doing so good that day. Everything'd just been building up. And he started talking about him and his mom leaving, and I kind of panicked, and I told him we'd talk in the morning, that we'd figure it out, but I knew he wasn't doing okay. I should've known he wouldn't go home."

"But you know where he is now," Mari jumps in.

"Yeah."

I tell them about the dam. I tell them about the trails we hiked when we all camped here, and about the little cave along the river.

"How do you know that's where he is?" Teagan asks.

I don't have a good answer. I just do. We've grown up together. Two tomato vines. The same kind of weird.

I know how Joel thinks.

"We have to go get him," Mari says.

"Should we tell the ranger?" Teagan asks. "Or Mom and Dad?"

But if Joel hears the whole group of us clomping through the woods looking for him—or, worse, if it's the park rangers or the police who go after him—will he hide? Will he worry that we'll try to bring him back to Riverview and go on like nothing's changed? Will he burrow deeper in the woods till even I can't find him?

"Not yet," I say. "Not all of them. Just us. We can bring him back."

I have no idea if Teagan's going to agree to that. But our parents are done with Ranger Sandra. They're telling her thanks for her help, that they're so grateful to have us home safe. Joel's mom stays back to talk to her longer, but my mom and dad and Mama Callie and Mama Elena are all heading our way.

They're going to drive us back to Riverview. It's all going to be over.

"We have a lot to talk about," my mom says when

they reach us. She clamps her hand on my shoulder, guiding me toward the doors. Out toward the parking lot. Teagan and Mari are both flashing wild eyes at me. "I am so glad you're safe, but I also cannot *believe* you ran off like that. When we get home—"

"Wait," I blurt out.

"What, sweet pea?" my dad says.

I slide out of my mom's grip. "I've got to use the bathroom first," I say.

They just stare at me. But I raise my eyebrows at Teagan and Mari, trying to send them a telepathy message.

Mari gets it immediately. "I've got to go, too," she says.

Come on, Teagan. I waggle my eyebrows harder at her.

"Me too," Teagan says.

My mom sighs, but my dad just shrugs. Mama Elena and Mama Callie exchange a look.

"Hurry, okay?" Mama Elena says. "They're getting ready to close up the visitor center."

They let us go. Teagan bumps her shoulder against

mine as we head toward the bathroom. It's a sign of trust. She's trusting that I know what I'm doing.

I don't usually like going into girls' bathrooms. It's just another place I feel like I don't fit, another place I feel outside myself. But I'm past caring about that right now. Mari, Teagan, and me all head into the girls' bathroom together.

ONE LAST ESCAPE PLAN

IT TURNS OUT THE ESCAPE ROUTE FROM INSIDE THE PUBLIC RESTROOM at the Mammoth Cave National Park visitor center is easy:

There's a window.

The window is narrow and up high on the wall, almost at the ceiling. It's cracked open just a little. A sweet, woodsy breeze floats in through it, getting all mixed up with the sour bathroom smells inside.

"I'll boost you up," I say right away. "We've only got a couple minutes before they come looking for us. We've got to go. *Now.*"

"No, *you* have to go," Teagan says.

I stare at her. I wait for Mari to argue, but she's nodding along.

"We'll stall them for you," Mari says. "We can buy you a couple extra minutes. But you're the one who knows where he is. You can get to him."

"Besides," Teagan says. "I do actually really have to pee."

Another time, that would make me laugh. But time is slipping away.

"Okay," I say.

Mari and Teagan thread their fingers together and make their hands into platforms for my sneakers. They boost me up to the window. One foot at a time. Clambering onto the windowsill feels like all those afternoons when Joel and me climbed over the fence by the science annex—one foot wedged in the chain links, hauling the other leg over the top. I push the window open as far as it will go, and for a second I'm sitting on the sill like it's a horse, straddling it. One leg dangling inside, one outside.

"You sure about this?" I ask.

With me blocking all the sunlight from the window,

it's just fluorescent bathroom lights on Teagan's and Mari's faces. Mari's expression is hard to read. But her eyes are glinting. "Completely sure."

"Just come back, okay?" Teagan says.

I nod. And maybe another time, that might've been a lie. I've spent so long wanting to just hide. Wanting to be someplace besides Riverview, someplace no one would see me. Now, though...

I look down at their faces. And I know they've both got my back.

And that's something.

I slide out the window.

I've spent so long figuring that I just had to play the part. Forever. That I'd teach myself the right and wrong topics to talk about. That I'd teach myself how to dress right and how to act right and how to be a nice young lady. That I'd get good at it, good enough that maybe someday no one besides me would even be able to tell the ways my pieces never quite fit into any of that.

I spent so long just running on what everybody around me figured I'd do that I started believing it. I started feeling like whatever they saw when they looked at me was more real than anything I felt. Like they were right and I was wrong.

But something about today has pushed me out of that. In the woods, there's nobody wanting you to do anything. Nobody expecting anything from you. Nobody even looking at you to see whatever outside version they see that doesn't feel right. It's just you and the trees and *you*.

Just me.

I drop from the window and hit hard on the balls of my feet. My sneakers squelch into the mud. It's not a far drop. Still, the landing makes my whole body jar. I feel it in my teeth. I feel it in my skull.

I take off running.

PART THREE

THE BOATHOUSE

IT'S BEEN YEARS SINCE MY FAMILY AND JOEL'S FAMILY STAYED IN THE cabin at Mammoth Cave. Years since we spent the whole week hiking these trails. I don't remember exactly which trail we took that day, the one that led us down to the Green River.

But as I start off along the paved path away from the visitor center, I can remember enough. I know which direction to go toward the river. I know that when I find the water, I'll follow it north, upstream. I dodge past a park ranger's tour group, probably coming back from the last tour of the day, and turn down a wide asphalt path that leads into the woods.

One of Mammoth Cave's main entrances is down this path, I remember, but the trailheads are, too. That week, this is where we started all our hikes.

As soon as I'm in the trees' shade, the humidity breaks. It's that time of day when the sweltering heat of the afternoon shifts to the breezier heat of evening. When you start finishing up your game because you know you're going to get called home to dinner soon. I take a huge breath of cool air. Let it out. Time my breaths with the pounding of my feet as I jog down the path. I don't know how long Teagan and Mari can stall our parents. Any minute now, they might come outside looking for me.

It's all downhill, though, and gravity does half the work. The farther I run, the more I get pulled along, faster and faster, until I feel like I'm disconnecting from the ground. I fly past a group of hikers. Fly past a family with two little kids, parents tying the kids' shoes while the kids fuss, probably cranky at the end of a long day.

I feel the main cave entrance before I see it: a puff of cool air, at least twenty degrees colder than the rest of the woods. The temperature inside Mammoth

Cave is almost always fifty-four degrees, year-round. I remember that from our school trips. In summer it feels cold; in winter it's practically warm.

Beside the path I'm running on, a staircase leads down, down, down until it disappears under the huge gap in the rock. The entrance opens up like a yawn. A shiver runs along my back, and it's not just from the cold.

The cave feels *alive*.

There's so much here underneath the surface. So much waiting to be explored.

I don't take the staircase, though. Not this time. Instead, I keep following the main path downhill as it winds deeper into the woods. When the path splits off into two different dirt trails, I try to picture the map of the park on the wall in Ranger Sandra's office. Try to get my bearings.

Find the river. Follow it upstream.

Then I see it and almost laugh: a sign carved with a picture of a canoe and the words *Boat Rentals*. An arrow pointing down the trail to the left.

I follow it.

My plan has been fuzzy as I ran away from the

center. Now, as I race through the trees—green and green and green—it becomes less of a plan and more of another confession. Almost a prayer.

Bless me, Father, for I have sinned. That's the first thing you say when you meet the priest for the sacrament of confession at church. It's the line that keeps running through my mind now, keeping pace with my footsteps. My lungs are burning. I'm grimy and sweaty from walking all day, and my feet are ready to fall off.

Bless me, Father, for today I set a fire inside a church.

Bless me, Father, for today I lied to my parents and roped my sister and my friend into lying to them, too.

The woods thin out up ahead, and the path ends at the rickety wooden boathouse. But *boathouse* isn't the right word. It's not a house. It's barely even a shed. It's a tiny square of a building with peeling paint on its walls and a little window cut into one side. Behind it, the river's surface sparkles in the evening sunlight.

I stop running, and for a second I can only clutch at the stabbing stitch in my side. Try to breathe. The boathouse window is empty this time of day. No rental attendant is here to take a fee or ask me where my parents are. No one is around at all. It's just me and the river.

A plastic rain barrel beside the boathouse holds paddles. On the grass all around, canoes and kayaks are propped upside down, their bottoms air-drying. Just sitting there.

Bless me, Father, for I'm about to steal a boat.

I pick the smallest canoe. Hopefully the easiest to steer. Probably the only one I can push into the water on my own. It's dented in a few places, and the red paint on its side has almost faded to pink. I heave it upright. Pick a paddle. Drag them both toward the river.

It's time to travel the same way Joel did.

I don't take the time to think. I don't take the time to plan it out. I just do. I nudge the canoe's nose out into the water, sliding through the mud of the riverbank. Step into the canoe. I teeter for a second, but then I catch myself and settle onto the seat. It's still damp from whenever its last renter used it. The river's current pushes against the front of the canoe, but the rest of the boat is still stuck in the mud, so I dig the paddle into the ground to try to push off.

The bottom of the canoe groans. It squelches. But I can feel the exact moment when the water takes hold and we're free of the bank.

And I'm off.

MYSTERIES

I STRUGGLE AGAINST THE CURRENT A LOT AT FIRST. THE RIVER ISN'T moving fast, but it's still enough to push my boat back. I can't find the rhythm of the paddle. I paddle a few times on one side and then switch to the other, like I've seen people do, but I keep steering myself sideways. I'm trying to go upstream, and the water's working against me. Sweeping me away.

And then somehow something clicks, and the rhythm falls into place. My paddling evens out. Each of my strokes starts to push me up the river, straightening out into a clear course. The river is still whispering like it has been all day. But now that I'm in its current, it's louder than ever: *RUSH. RUSH. RUSH.* My paddle dips in and out of the water, a whispering sound of its own.

Once I've gotten the hang of paddling, the canoe cuts through the water smoothly. Everything else falls away. The forest. The sky. My parents back at the visitor center. Now, for the first time, I can feel this journey the way Joel might have felt it. I can feel the way the current gently pushes at my boat. I can feel the shadow of the trees high overhead, the coolness on my face when their shade blocks out the late-afternoon sunlight. I can skim my palm along the surface of the water, cold and green and bracing, and I can feel the river ripple around me.

But it's all different, too. The canoe glides instead of chopping through the water the way our blocky raft would. I'm pushing it upstream, while Joel would've been letting the current carry him down. And I didn't make this boat. Not like we made the raft.

This *isn't* how Joel felt.

I *can't* feel how Joel felt.

When you pray the rosary, you're not just listing off the prayers. Whatever Joel might say. The rosary isn't just a checklist of Our Fathers and Hail Marys. Every time you pray it, you're supposed to meditate on one part of Jesus's story—a part that's hard to understand, or maybe *impossible* to understand. A part that maybe doesn't make total sense. A part that maybe feels a little like pretend sometimes. A part that, in the end, you've just got to take on faith.

We memorized all of them in Sunday school. All the different parts of the story that you're supposed to meditate on while you pray the rosary. Each one of them is called a mystery.

You can study them and think about them and pray the rosary every day, and they'll still be mysteries. There are still parts of the story you won't understand. You're supposed to keep studying anyway. And keep meditating. And keep praying. And keep *trying*. But you're not going to understand everything. You can't.

As much as I've wanted to believe I can lay out all the reasons Joel left, I can't.

I like having clean answers. I wanted to be able to make a list of reasons. To make them make sense. Some of his reasons I understand, but not all of them.

There are parts of Joel's story, parts of Joel being Joel, that I can think about and learn more about and *believe* when he tells me. I can listen to what he needs. I can speak up when he needs me to.

But I'm never going to fully, 100 percent understand Joel's reasons. I'll keep trying. I'll keep working. But as tied together as we are—as much as we've grown up together—he's not me. And I'm not him.

I dig my paddle into the water, and I push my canoe forward, and I think about Mari and Teagan back at the visitor center, covering for me. I think about my mom and dad. They might not always know the right way to help. They might be better at pretending everything's all right than at fixing it when it's not. But they can learn to try. I think about Mama Callie and about Mama Elena and her hand on my shoulder this morning.

I've got so many people who have my back. People who I can talk to. People who I can tell the pieces to, when I'm ready.

And I think about Joel's mom back at the visitor center, too. About her looking for Joel in all the towns around Riverview. About her pulling me aside after church, trying to find out any piece she possibly could that might help her find him.

The river whispers, *Rush, rush, rush.* It whispers, *Go, go, go.*

I go.

FINDING JOEL

FINALLY, THE RIVER STARTS TO BEND. THE WOODED HILL ON MY LEFT grows into a cliff. The layers of rock tower above me and my canoe.

I can see the dark opening in the rock up ahead.

Compared with the main Mammoth Cave entrance I ran past earlier, this miniature cave is nothing. Just a small archway sloping into the rock wall. Probably the cave inside it doesn't even go twenty feet back. Probably it doesn't even have any cave beetles.

But Joel had promised the two of us would come back here.

I steer the canoe toward the rocky bank. Hear

the grinding sound as the bottom hits land. I'll have to get out to pull it ashore, though, so I untie my shoelaces and peel off my sneakers and socks. Just like Joel and I did that first day when we built fairy rafts in Mystic Creek. I leave my shoes in the bottom of the boat and swing my bare feet over the side and into the ankle-deep shallows. The water is *cold*. It's so cold it bites. I drag the canoe farther up onto the shore, and when that stops working I go around behind it and push, push, until it's nosed far enough up onto the bank that it won't drift away.

I stand there and take it all in. Rock wall looming up above me. Trees high overhead, their branches making a cathedral ceiling of leaves. River lapping at the stones under my feet.

The cave pulls me toward it. Everything's quiet.

"Joel?" I say.

My voice sounds small. Swallowed up by the woods.

"Joel? Are you here?"

I walk barefoot right up to the entrance of the cave. Peek through the gloom. There's a little pool of water in a dip in the rock just inside. The jagged walls narrow and disappear into the dark. I can't see the back.

I just stand outside, looking in. My heart's thundering in my chest. After all that time I spent begging my dad to let us go explore it—after this whole day of following Joel—I'm afraid to go inside by myself.

"Joel?" My voice echoes.

No one answers.

And finally I have to ask it: What if he's not here?

What if I'm wrong?

How could I be wrong? I found the trail markers. I felt the pull. I felt the river connecting us, that tin-can-telephone string. Everything felt *right*.

What am I supposed to do if he's not here? Go back to the visitor center? Explain everything to my parents and get grounded for the rest of my life? Look Joel's mom in the eye yet again and admit to her that yes, I lied to her, I thought I knew where he was and I didn't tell her—but that it doesn't matter anyway, because I was wrong?

I don't have a plan for after this. All my plans ended here. All my plans ended with Joel here.

I miss him.

"Hey," I say into the cave.

It feels silly at first. It feels silly to be talking out loud, talking into this cave, when it's empty. When Joel isn't here. It feels like playing a game, like praying, like pretending but all the while having an itching suspicion that it's not real.

But I'm in the woods. We've been playing pretend in the woods for my whole life, and our games of pretend have always been real in some ways. They've always still meant something.

"Hey, Joel," I say again.

And then I'm just talking.

"I'm sorry. I mean, I'm sorry for everything. For not standing up for you. And for not knowing what to say. And for being kind of an awful friend when you needed me. I'm sorry I didn't talk to you that night when we were out camping—that I didn't know what you needed. And I'm sorry I didn't want to listen when you were trying to *tell* me what you needed."

The words are flowing out of me, flowing like the river. But no one answers. The cave is empty.

I turn away from it and pick my way barefoot

301

across the bank, back to the river. A wide, flat rock hangs over the water, and I sit down on it. Feel my feet aching from all the miles we walked today. I let them dangle in the water, freezing and so murky that when I look down I can barely see my own toes. The water around them swirls with green. It's a weird feeling, having a part of me someplace I can't see.

But even as I sit there, my feet *stop* feeling like part of me—they're so cold they're going numb. Even though I see them, it's like they stop existing.

I breathe in the woodsy smell. I breathe in the sweetness of leaves and the river breeze and the sticky humidity of central Kentucky in the beginning of summer. The sun is dropping lower in the sky, making the tops of the trees glow gold.

The water laps at my ankles. Looking at it, you would barely even notice it's moving, but I can feel it—I can feel the current sliding along my skin. It's just a tug. It's light and faint, just a suggestion, but it suggests a clear direction. Any way I turn my feet, I can feel the tug pulling.

I look back against the current, toward Riverview: toward the woods Joel and I play in and the garden where I help my dad grow tomatoes and the high brick steeple of the Church of the Sacred Heart, somewhere far away through those trees.

And then I look the direction the current goes. Where the Green connects with the Ohio. Where the Ohio hits the Mississippi. Where the Mississippi empties out into the Gulf of Mexico. And from there… *everywhere.*

It's all so big. My eyes start to prickle again, and there's the lump in my throat that comes right before tears, because I don't know. I don't know what to do. There are pieces I've been putting together today… for a while now, really. Pieces about who I am. Pieces about who I want to be.

Because I don't want to be a girl.

I don't think I *am* a girl.

I let myself think it: *I'm not a girl.* I swallow, and I blink, and my eyes are wet, and the tears start to spill out. Maybe it's exciting to finally admit that. Even just to myself. But it's also terrifying. It's too much. It feels like something is growing in my chest, warm and fragile and scared, and it grows and grows until it's too big to hold inside. So it starts to spill out.

I don't know how to do this.

I know Joel isn't here. But talking to him helps anyway. My voice shakes a little. "I just really need you right now," I say. "And I think you need me, too. Maybe in different ways. Maybe for a different reason. But...can we just talk?"

I'm not expecting an answer.

Except that then a stick somewhere behind me cracks. And footsteps shuffle along the rocks. And a figure is climbing around the corner of the bluff, with a stretched-out T-shirt and dark curly hair gone even curlier in the humidity.

"Aubrey?"

If I wasn't already crying, I'd start now. It's like seeing Joel here in real life has released something in me. I'm on my feet. Scrabbling over the rocky bank. Running toward him as he runs toward me. Then we're hugging. I've never been much of a hugging person, but I hug Joel. I hug the heck out of him.

"You found me," he says with his face pressed into my shoulder. "How did you find me? How did you *get* here?"

"I stole a canoe," I say. My face is pressed into *his* shoulder, too. The words come out muffled.

"What?"

"Long story."

I pull back for a second to wipe my eyes. I take him in: Joel, who's looking rumpled and smelling like a campfire, but with a grin on his face I've seen a million times before. He's taking me in, too. For once, I'm okay with that.

"I was leaving you trail markers," he says. "The whole way here. I didn't really think you'd find them, though. I didn't really think..."

He shakes his head. That wild grin splits his face again.

"Why'd you leave them, then?" I say.

"I guess I hoped."

We make our way back to the cave hand in hand. He shows me what I would have found if I'd ventured a little farther inside: tucked into the back corner, nestled in the dark, is his backpack and sleeping bag. He's got a flashlight and a paper with the last of his food, whatever's left from our camping trip back in

Riverview. Two field guides are flipped open on his sleeping bag, ones he borrowed from me so long ago I forgot he had them.

"I've started exploring," he says. "Seeing if I could find berries or plants that are safe to eat around here."

"Did you find any?" I ask.

"Nah." But he doesn't look too upset about it. "I did find one of those punk black-and-white butterflies! The striped zebratail!"

"Zebra swallowtail," I tell him. And then I add, "I missed you." Because I'm learning to say the things I mean. I'm learning to say things out loud when they might help someone.

"I missed you, too," he says.

"I have so much to tell you," I say.

"Me too," he says.

And so we do.

THE END OF THE DAY

JOEL AND ME SIT DOWN ON MY ROCK OVER THE RIVER AND TALK FOR A long, long while. Just like we've always sat and talked in the woods. We dangle our feet in the water. Around us, the trees are turning yellow and gold in the setting sunlight. The nighttime crickets are starting to chirp.

We talk about everything that's happened—not just today, but this year. I tell him my apologies. I tell him I'm going to try harder. That I want to know what's going on with him and that I'm going to pay more attention.

"Some of the things you were saying...that night,"

I say. It feels dangerous and fragile to talk about the last night I saw him. Part of me wants to pretend it never happened. But that's not how friendship works. "I know you said you're not…what Rudy Thomas called you."

I take a breath. I can say it. It's not a bad word.

"Gay," I say. "I know you said you weren't gay. And I believe you. But I've been thinking, and I don't know how to—" I breathe again. "I might be?" I say.

"Oh," Joel says.

"Not gay exactly. I mean, I don't know. It's not that I *like*-like girls, exactly. I don't even know *who* I like-like." I'm rambling. I'm doing this all wrong. But Joel is looking at me carefully, and he's smiling. He doesn't hate me; he doesn't think I'm wrong. He's smiling at me, just like he always has. "I mean, I don't think *I'm* a girl."

I'm crying again, and Joel wraps his arms around my shoulders. "Hey," he's saying. "It's okay. It's okay, A. Like, you're trans? You might be a boy?"

Him hugging me is just making me cry harder. The tears are spilling out of me right alongside the words I've been so sure I could never talk about.

I *can* talk about this, it turns out. I can talk about this, and I can still have people love me when I do.

"I don't know," I'm saying. "I don't even know. Maybe a boy? Or maybe not? Maybe I'm not a 'he' or 'she' kind of a person? I don't know. I don't know how to know. There's just so…*much*, and—"

"It's okay, A! It's okay." His hand rubs up and down on my shoulder, keeping me warm. "I knew there was something bothering you. I could tell. I just didn't know what. But you don't have to know all the answers right now. Right? You don't have to know everything."

Joel knows how I *want* to know everything. He knows how I like to line up all the pieces and list things out. He knows I like to have names for every tree and leaf and animal. So he knows how hard the not-knowing is for me.

But he's still just going to be here. Waiting with me. Letting me figure it out.

I don't have any tissues, so I wipe my runny nose on my hand. Joel holds out his T-shirt sleeve for me. I wipe my snotty hand on his shirt.

"You're disgusting," he tells me.

But he's grinning.

"And I hope I'm not stealing the show," he adds. "With the big announcements and all. But I think I am, actually. I *am* gay. So. That's a thing."

He's looking at me a little sideways, waiting for my reaction, and there's so many things I'm going to tell him: that I love him, that I'm here for him, that I'm glad he can say it, too. I'll say it in a minute, though. Sometimes, actions speak louder.

I tackle hug him, and we both tumble over sideways on the rock, laughing.

We've been secrets, both of us, and somehow we didn't realize that we didn't have to be. That's the thing about secrets: Sometimes, once you've stopped keeping the secret from yourself, it doesn't have to be a secret at all. You just have to tell one person.

We're straightening up, letting our bare feet slide back into the water, when Joel spots something in the shallows and leans forward, his face somehow lit even brighter with excitement.

"Oh, hey again, little buddy," he says.

My heart stops when I see what he's talking to. A long, muscular body draped over a rock by his ankles. Brown bands down its scaly back. Coppery brown head.

"Get away from that!" I yelp.

Joel and the snake both look up at me, startled. I'm reeling with the whiplash of going from absolute relief to absolute terror. It's the same kind of snake Mari and I saw by the river earlier this afternoon. I know it is.

"It's okay," Joel tells me, still too calm. "This little guy's been hanging around here since this morning."

"It's a copperhead!" I get out, and my voice squeaks. "Venomous!"

"I thought that, too, at first, but it's okay, A. It's... just a sec."

He holds up one finger for me to wait, as if I can do anything else, as if I can do anything besides keep staring at the snake below us in the shallows. The snake keeps staring at me, too. Joel takes off into the cave, and a second later he comes back with one of my field guides. He flips through the pages.

"Here," he says. My heart's still pounding, but I tear my eyes away from the real-life snake and let him show me a page of snake photographs instead.

"'Northern water snake,'" he reads out, jabbing his finger at one of the pictures. "See how its head is rounder, like this one? Copperheads have more of a triangle head, it turns out. And their bands are different shapes."

I've looked at the diagrams on these pages dozens of times, but when Mari and I saw the snake earlier, I was too frozen with fear to remember any of them. But sure enough, the more I look back and forth between the snake at our feet and the photos in the book, the more obvious it gets that it's not a copperhead at all. The brown bands on the snake's back match the water snake picture exactly. I breathe, and my heart starts slowing back to a normal speed. I breathe again.

"This says people get them confused a lot," Joel is saying. "They'll try to hurt a water snake thinking it's a copperhead, when really they should just let it do its thing."

The water snake has gotten bored of us by now. It slithers back toward the edge of the island, curling in and out of the tall grasses at the water's edge.

The orange sunlight shimmers on the snake's scales. Now that I know it's not going to hurt us, it's kind of beautiful.

"I can't believe I had to explain that to *you*, of all people," he says, plopping back down beside me. "You're the one who taught *me* how to identify all this stuff!"

"Shut up," I say, but I'm smiling.

"You good?"

"Yeah."

And I am now. It feels like it's finally going to be okay.

The snake keeps slithering around in the shallows as Joel and I sit and talk, watching the sun getting lower in the sky.

He tells me about his past three days: about taking the raft that night, after our fight, when he was restless and frustrated and didn't see another option. When he just had to get out. He tells me about floating along the river, letting the current take him.

He tells me about what it feels like to have no real control over how fast you're going or *where* you're going. He tells me about what it feels like to be on a raft, alone, floating down the river. What the trees sound like. What the water feels like.

He tells me about camping out, alone, along the riverbank. About leaving the trail markers.

"I still can't believe you found me," he says. "I mean, I *can* believe it—I hoped you would—but...I don't know. Maybe I didn't think you'd want to."

I look him square in the eyes. I don't have a name for the face he's making. Or maybe I don't need a name for it. But his chin's ducked a little, anxious, waiting.

"It doesn't matter where you go," I tell him. "You're not getting rid of me. Not ever."

We haven't yet brought up what comes next. Because we both know the truth of it. The truth is that we can't stay out here. We can't just disappear into the woods. I've spent so long not wanting to be in Riverview, or not wanting to be *me*, but that's not something I can walk away from. It's a part of me.

And maybe it's a part of me that I can start to find the right words for. I've got people around me I can talk to. People who will have my back. I think I'm ready for whatever comes next, more ready than I've ever been.

And Joel can't just stay out here forever, foraging off wild berries, camping in the woods. It doesn't work that way. Not in real life.

But we can't go back to the way things were, either.

We can't go back to Riverview and pretend everything's just the same. We can't *let* it be the same. I don't want to start seventh grade this way—with Rudy Thomas still saying the things he's said, with the vice principal still not doing anything about it, with Joel still not fitting. Not at school, not at home.

I don't want Joel to feel wrong. I want him to feel right, because he is.

"My mom," Joel says.

"I know," I say. "She's back at the visitor center. She was out here looking for you. Just like we were."

He swallows hard. "Was my dad?"

I don't know whether Joel is hoping the answer is yes or no. I just shake my head.

"I'm gonna ask to go to Louisville with my mom," he says.

"I know," I say. It hurts my stomach to say it. But it's the right choice.

"My Aunt Reesa is pretty cool. She's said before that she'd let us stay with her for a while. When my mom and dad have talked about, you know. Separating. I don't think we'll stay there forever. But for now."

He's picking at a scab on his knee, scratching his fingernails on skin. I put my hand over his just for a second, and he stops.

"I think it's for the best," Joel says.

"I think it is, too. But I'm gonna miss you."

"It's only a couple hours' drive. I can see you on weekends."

"Yeah, well. I'll still miss you."

We're intertwined tomato vines, peas in a pod. But in the end, we're different people, Joel and me. Similar but not the same. We're going to keep making our friendship work. Even if that means going our separate ways sometimes. Even if that means that sometimes we need different things.

Finally, when the air starts to get cool in the way it does at the end of a long summer day, Joel stands up. He offers me a hand and pulls me to my feet.

"Ready to go home?" he says.

And I am.

NEXT MONTH

ON A FRIDAY EVENING, AFTER I'VE HELPED MY MOM WASH UP THE DINNER dishes and shut myself in my room, I sneak out through my bedroom window. The outside air is hot, but the humidity of the afternoon is starting to break. It's still light out, though—one of those drawn-out summer evenings, the kind that used to make Joel and me beg and beg our parents to let us keep playing outside for a couple more hours after dinnertime.

Bugs nip at my legs as I jog up the sidewalk toward Joel's house. Even from halfway down the street, I can spot the Gallaghers' car parked in the driveway, all loaded up with suitcases.

Joel and his mom head to Louisville tomorrow morning. He's been packing and unpacking all week, trying to decide which clothes to take, and it's all more complicated because they don't know how long they're going to stay. His mom and dad have been talking a lot, Joel says, but there's just so much they haven't decided on yet. They haven't decided yet how long they're going to separate. They haven't decided if Joel is coming back here for the new school year.

"We're all still figuring it out," he told me when we were hanging out earlier this afternoon. Then he'd nudged my leg with the toe of his sneaker and smiled, because I'm still figuring some things out, too, I guess.

Instead of knocking on the front door, I loop around to the back of the house. Joel's bedroom window is lit up. I'm just about to tap my fingers on the glass when I peek through it and realize he's not alone. I snatch my hand back. I hold my breath.

Joel's mom is in the doorway of his room. She's leaning against the frame, telling him something and moving her hands around a lot as she talks—just like Joel does. Joel's room is the cleanest I've ever seen

319

it. He's zipping up his old school backpack with a few things, and then he hands it to his mom and tells her good night.

Before she goes, she kisses him on top of his head, pressing it into his curls.

I wait till the door's closed behind her and Joel's alone before I drum my fingers on the window. When Joel sees me, his face breaks into a huge smile I've started calling his Crinkle-Eyed Grin. He practically flies across the room to fling the window open.

"About time!" he says.

"Shh!" I hiss.

"Oh! Right." He lowers his voice to a stage whisper. "About time!"

"It's not even late," I tell him. "You ready?"

"Wait, I've got something for you! Just a sec," he says, and takes off out of the room at a dead sprint.

Ten seconds pass while I stare at the empty window and slap at a mosquito that's found my arm. Then Joel sprints back in holding a Tupperware box high up above his head like it's got the crown jewels inside. He presses the box into my hands.

"My mom and I made them," he says. "But I forgot to give them to you earlier."

Inside the box is a row of chocolate cupcakes, all with gloppy icing tops coated in sprinkles and edible glitter and chocolate chips.

"We baked them from scratch," Joel tells me, and he's smiling so proud of himself that I smile, too.

"Of course you did. It's about the *process*, right?"

"Eat one, tell me how good they are!"

I dig in. They really are good. Way better than the rubbery burnt ones we kept making months ago, during Joel's first cupcake phase. I'm glad he's cycled back around to baking again. The decorations aren't tidy or fancy, but they're very Joel, so I love them.

Joel eats one, too, and then we click the Tupperware shut again, and I tuck it under my arm to take with us.

"That's smart," Joel says, nodding. "Provisions."

We won't be gone long, though. Not this time. Joel's leaving tomorrow, but neither of us wanted him to go before we found a way to mark his last night in Riverview. We haven't decided how we'll mark it, exactly, but we'll figure it out, just like everything else. We invited Mari, too. She's going to meet us in the woods.

I help Joel pop the mosquito screen out of the window frame, and he slides through feetfirst. He lands beside me on the grass.

"You ready?" I ask him again. And this time, he is. We take off running into our woods.

Away, away, away.

ACKNOWLEDGMENTS

This book has been many years in the making, and it could never have made the journey from my heart onto the pages here without the help of so many people.

First, thank you to my outstanding agent, Beth Phelan, for being incredibly patient and understanding but also ready to push me when I need it, for answering all my ridiculous questions, and for guiding me through every step of this process. Beth is an amazing advocate, and I'm grateful every day to get to be on her team.

Thank you to my editor, Nikki Garcia, who asked all the right questions and pointed out all the right places to dig deeper. Your keen editorial eye helped shape this into a stronger story than I ever thought it could be, and I appreciate your support so much.

Thank you to Celia Krampien for creating this book's beautiful cover and capturing Aubrey and Joel's world so well. Thank you to Karina Granda and Patrick Hulse for the design; production editor Marisa Finkelstein; copy editor Erica Ferguson; marketing manager Bill Grace; digital marketing specialist Mara Brashem; school and library marketing coordinator Christie Michel; publicist Cheryl Lew; and the entire team at Little, Brown Books for Young Readers for helping this story find its readers.

I've had some fantastic opportunities in the writing community so far and am so grateful for all the writers I've gotten to connect with. Thank you to Julian Winters for your thoughtful insights and absolutely spot-on recommendations. Thank you to PitchWars and especially to my wonderful mentors, Nicole Melleby and A. J. Sass, for all of your edit notes, cheerleading, and hand-holding along the way. Thank you to Lambda Literary for building a truly life-changing program through your Writer's Retreat for Emerging LGBTQ Voices. Thanks to emily danforth for your faith in my story and the stories of everyone in our workshop, and an enormous thank-you to our whole Lambda cohort: I'm constantly in awe of all of you. Thanks especially to Jen St. Jude, Jas Hammonds, and Kirt Ethridge for lending your energy reading drafts of this book (and to Kirt for first bringing up the mysteries of the rosary during workshop!).

Thank you always and forever to Natalie Morgan, ultimate cheerleader, who's been with me on this journey from the very beginning, and to Katherine Ouellette, who's kept me on track with our coffee-shop-turned-video-chat accountability sessions and made the writing process so much less solitary.

Huge shout-out to my siblings, Megan, Kate, Kevin, and Tricia: Thanks for all those games of pretend in the backyard and basement when we were growing up. And to my parents: Thank you for your faith in me when I told you I wanted to be a writer, even when I hadn't shown you anything I'd been writing for eighteen years. I'm so grateful that I can share my stories joyfully with you now.

Finally, thank you to my wife, Cara, the best person I know. I don't have to be a secret with you. I love you so much.